I0726684

STILLPOINT

A Novel

George Ovitt

Fomite
Burlington, Vemont

This is a work of fiction. Any resemblance between the characters of these stories and real people, living or dead, is merely coinci- dental.

Copyright 2018 © George Ovitt
Cover image: "Old Woman Reading", Sándor Galimberti, 1907
ISBN-13: 978-1-944388-65-2
Library of Congress Control Number: 2018955402

Fomite
58 Peru Stree
Burlington, VT 05401
www.fomitepress.com

For Brigid

*Nascevi ai dolci sogni intanto, e il primo/
Sole splendeati in vista*

Leopardi, "Ad Angelo Mai"

"How does your mind employ itself? This is the whole issue. All else, of your own choice or not, is corpse and smoke."
Marcus Aurelius (12:33)

"At the still point of the turning world. Neither flesh nor fleshless;
Neither from nor towards; at the still point, there the dance is,
But neither arrest nor movement."
T. S. Eliot, Burnt Norton

Morning

Elle thought of herself as being on dawn patrol. She'd always been an early riser, thinking nothing of being in the kitchen with her first cup of coffee at 5 a.m., long before the sun had breached the vast plain on whose western rim she lived. One of the concessions Elle had made to old age was "sleeping in," or, as she put it to her son in a recent letter, "I've started to lounge around in the mornings, lying in until nearly 6 as I did when I was a girl." Six seemed self-indulgent, so Elle would force herself out of bed and into her robe and slippers a few minutes before so that she could maintain the fiction of early rising. It wasn't easy. Her body, not much catered to over the course of seven decades, preferred to remain where it was, and Elle, a dreamy, solitary woman, enjoyed those first moments of wakefulness, the silence of the house, memories that crept unbidden from her dreams. On the other hand, there was work to be done and little time left to do it.

"After all," she told Todd, "my father would have done half a day's work by nine," which wasn't close to being true, but Elle was no more immune to mythologizing her life than anyone. "Dawn patrol," a metaphor derived from hot air ballooning—a popular past-time in these parts—was Elle's term for the hour of idleness she spent with her coffee, watching the gathering light outside her large east-facing window.

This morning, like every morning since her retirement from Harris and Twitchell, Elle put a record on the turntable. Something straightforward—Bach's orchestral suites—then she added kindling and piñon logs to the enormous cast-iron stove whose waning heat was, at this hour, barely keeping the frost from the windows. Chilled and caffeinated, she sat in her ancient rocker, mildly engaged with the slow turning of the earth. "Pitching the sun into view," or "watching the world come into the light," a Quaker formulation she'd heard years before in Washington D.C.'s Meeting House, passivity and quiet observation being the Friends' way. Elle imagined the great wheel of the universe pushing her small house out of the darkness, "As if I were settled on the edge of a pinwheel," like the ones she would make at summer camp, pinwheels and origami cranes, lanyards and bracelets of frayed wool. Sixty years ago, "good with her hands," as her mother put it, an oblique compliment since "good with one's hands" meant not so good with one's mind, the mechanical arts suspect to those who had risen to respectability, or to those who preferred to pay others to do their chores for them. Yes, it had been—could she recall?—Camp Something or other. Pinecrest? Pine Bough? Always camps were piney, worn-out log cabins tucked into shady pine-strewn woods full of mosquitos and poison ivy. Air reeking of summer and mildew. In any case, Elle had crafted keepsakes, junk that her mother stowed for a few days in the kitchen drawer before quietly, discreetly, (Elle had been a terrible packrat), tossing them in the trash. Nick-knacks and memories being indulgences that were unaffordable once Father had left. Elle smiled at the word "Father," thinking of how her mother had never referred to her husband in any other way, not in Elle's hearing, always it was *Father*, the capital letter implied, as if Elle's meek *Daddy* was a medieval lord. "Your Father," never "my husband." No endearments in that house. Language opening and closing the heart with equal felicity.

Outside her "grand window" it was cold and clear, as it would be every day during January, the thin air moved by the tail end of the Rockies toward the flattened landscape of Estancia. In the clear mornings the wind barely rippled the Buddhist prayer flags Elle had tied to the eaves of her house. By mid-afternoon they would snap and flutter in the rush of air southward, perhaps, she imagined, toward the unbroken stretch of beach at Todos Santos. She allowed the memory of Baja to distract her for a few moments, the endless white sand, the tame breakers that slapped against her thighs. Elle hoped to keep her mind clear for the hour before she began work, as clear and empty as the turquoise sky, but it wasn't always possible to do so, to shut out thoughts that she would welcome later in the day. The trouble was, once she gave in even a little his words came flooding in, rushing to the fill the quiet in just the way the cold air from the north rushed to fill the space left by the rising warmth—when that happened, when his words started, Elle would have no rest. It might be days before she could still her mind to this point, to where she was fully herself, an old woman rocking in the dim light, sipping coffee, dreaming of a distant beach, intent upon silence.

There. The ravens were a nice distraction. How did they make those heavy bodies pirouette above the cottonwoods? Was there a way to put it? *Dare al vento precititi*…I suppose, Elle thought, they do seem thrown by the wind, like me, thrown into this life, of all the lives that might have been, or no life whatsoever. The accident of living, the luck of it. He would have an elegant way of putting this notion, *il destino invitto e la ferrata/ Necessita*, something something, I'll need to look but please not now, *Hard fate and iron necessity*, but is it so? Is it really thus that I am in this rocker, my coffee growing cold, the ravens tossed, the sky brightening enough so that I can make out details: the Dorothea Lange prints, the Gordon Parks, the reddening stove, photos of Elliot and of Todd on the mantle, the pattern in this carpet I bought in Beirut—or Cairo? I can't recall. Worn to the soul of the wool, plain brown, like me, worn to the plain brown of my soul. Elle lost the thought. She was wondering if it were true that we are thrown into the world and ruled not by our will but by chance. He thought so, he wrote it over and over, but his life led him to think so, his Catholic sadness. Elle unknotted her fingers. The tips were frayed this way and that, the joints swollen and painful. I'll need to take a pill. I need to hold the pen today. I can talk into the tape recorder, but writing is best.

First light—the cottonwoods catch it and brighten, a few lingering brown leaves turn to gold. Strange that they should hang on so long. What is it called? Abscission, *escissione*, they shuck off what isn't needed as if it were dead skin—leaves and fruit and bits of bark, entire branches—abscission, related to scissors, paring away, the prairie winds slicing at them, they know when the sun will be too weak, too absent, *fotosintesi*. Elle pushed up out of the chair and slipped into her houseshoes, horseshoes more like it, cloggy thick with muffed wool, her feet always cold on the wooden floors, worn-out oak, *not veneer*, easy to keep clean but "like ice." Her mother had said *her* heart, hers not Elle's, was "like ice," meaning, Elle supposed, not subject to emotion, as if emotion was something that came from outside, like sunlight. Her mother had been icy. Her skin hot in the way cold things are, burning. Five feet four inches tall. Diminutive, yet fearsome. Elle had inherited the short stature but lacked—luckily—the fearsomeness. What was the word for her, the exact word that came to mind when, as now, unbidden, her mother's face, long gone, presented itself? Daunting.

Her mother's English had been—difficult to use the past tense—full of music, Sienese, though she was born in Northeast Philadelphia—"In a row house on Macomb Avenue next door to a nice family restaurant"—and, "Your grandmother delivered me on the very bed on which your father and I made you." Elle had often wondered if it were true, about the bed, a story always told with the sharp vowels and elongated cadences that crept into her mother's dreamier moments, her monologues. Like many second-generation immigrants—Elle thought this on not much evidence—her mother had been able to shift linguistic gears seamlessly, from unaccented American English to a mix of Italian and barely recognizable and often misappropriated English—the bed of Elle's engendering and birth was always *"il letto"* but every other bed was just that—and Elle imagined that Cristina held onto her own mother's first language deliberately, out of affection, and not from sloppiness. Cristina—now that she was dead Elle felt less uncomfortable using her mother's given name—was compact in body and economical in speech and movement, as if wasting words or gestures was wasting money, something she would never do. Her mother's family had been working-class Philadelphians, not poor but not rich, "with one foot in the poorhouse," Elle's grandfather a SEPTA bus driver, her grandmother, when she worked at all, a housecleaner and family cook. Neither had finished high school. Cristina, intent upon her daughter's self-improvement, hadn't gone to college, though, as she often pointed out, everyone had said she could have. Their house had been one of the thousands of identical brick rowhouses built or refurbished in the 1940's, Philadelphia's Levittown, cheap homes for ex-GI's and their families, sturdy no-frills two-story fully-attached "three and two's" for Italian, Polish, Irish, German, and some Jewish families, all self-segregated by country of origin, mocking the fantastical notion of an American melting pot, keeping alive the tribalism that had brought them to the New World in the first place. America not a friendly place, no open arms for the dusky races. You might come to labor, but never—*never*—leave your ghetto. "We kept with our own kind." Good advice that Elle refused to follow.

The kitchen stove was blazing, the blue kettle steaming the frosted windows above the sink. Dried flowers—asters and sprigs of violets—shed onto the countertop where Elle stirred her coffee and pushed her mother away.

It was getting more difficult to do the same with his words—*Col suo fascio dell'erba; e reca in mano/Un mazzolin di rose e di viole*—that one had stumped her yesterday: "The young girl holding (*clutching?*) a bunch of violets and roses." The opening lines had given Elle fits—was the mood pastoral or melancholy? It was difficult to tell, impossible to separate her mood from his, to avoid the trap of adding her feelings to his. She poured a second cup of coffee, her final cup of the day. Her tachycardia might run on uncontrolled as she sat peering into dictionaries through the morning. More than two cups would make her jittery and keep her from concentrating. She'd be running to the bathroom when she needed to be writing. Elle stood over the sink staring blankly though the frosted glass. There was the snow-tipped buffalo grass sloping toward Slow Creek, actually No Creek since water hadn't flowed across the broken stones of the arroyo for three years, not since Elliot had died, three years— had they felt short or long? Long as lived, short in memory—Elle said, aloud, *unbelievable*, thinking as she said the word that it was not the right one to describe the death of a loved one. Words must always pass beyond belief to something more serious—*unbearable*, she said, and that seemed better, though untrue. Elliot was over there, in the flat pan of rocky earth that lay amid the unlikely elms, the ones that had been dying for nearly two decades. In summer it was the coolest place to sit, though when the rains came in August the flies drove you inside. A carved headstone, and a cairn, pointing the way toward the battered white house atop Granite Knoll, the name Elle had picked when she and Eliot arrived that first year of Bush Junior. The election was stolen, they said, the millennium likely to cause chaos, they said, the economy growing or shrinking, they said—who were *they*? Elle could never quite recall the details that filled the *Times* and NPR—she took the paper still, though she seldom read it, full as it was of trivia, fashion, and ads for movies she'd never see, and food—when exactly had food become such a preoccupation? And the radio, the urgency of events that were forgotten overnight. Of course she had no television. What was the point of paying attention to the world? Everything fell away so quickly, leaving no trace. The collective memory was full of half-truths; her countrymen liked it that way. Living where she did, being alone, Elle chose ignorance. Anyway, time was a jumble, her memory a dimming light. There were days when Elle stood where she was standing now, the spot she had stood for enough hours to wear a hole in the black linoleum, trying to remember something of no consequence: what shirt had Elliot worn on the day of Todd's wedding? What had he given her for Christmas the year of their marriage? Had they been happy? Elle didn't regard clawing after the debris of the past as a sign of senility but rather as proof of "functioning," a word she'd scribbled on a piece of foolscap and taped to the wall above her desk, just "functioning." The lowest common denominator of a sensible life entailed carrying on, doing work that perhaps had no meaning, but then, what did? "Why does it matter"—she insisted to herself, "it" being unallied to any noun in the world—"What does it matter," meaning exactly the opposite of what the words said—in fact, "it" mattered a great deal, whatever it was.

Not the button-down, so it must have been the full-on cotton shirt, the one I bought at Saks. He couldn't stop his hands from shaking long enough to put those little plastic tabs in the collar. Elle had to run to the study for one of her dictionaries because she couldn't recall if the word was "tab" or something else, and it turned out they were actually "stays," but also "knuckles" or "stiffeners" in England, where men knew a thing or two about dress shirts. But it wasn't the wedding or the shirt or the stay that preoccupied Elle on the day of Todd's wedding—his second marriage Elle thought, or perhaps his third—not the first for sure, not to Bess, doomed Bess, but to what's her name, the Irish-French woman, Gilly, plain Gil, short for Gilberte, her father French, or her mother, one of them having grown up, Elle thought, in Arles or Rouen, some place not Paris. Todd fell for the dark ones. "Tresses," *capigliatura*, a glistening head full of raven-black, black-blue hair. A raven in the light wasn't black at all, but a shiny blue that was nearly iridescent. Todd would sit next to her, to

Gilly, on the couch—it must have been in Boston—and run his hands through her unconstrained hair and pretend to have become tangled, and to pull her, plain Gil, toward him. She wasn't plain, Elle remembered how lovely she was, not plain but plain-spoken, some kind of scientist, a botanist, always off on what she called "research trips," traipsing through forests in Costa Rica, sailing up or down the Amazon, an adventure Elle couldn't imagine, Gil speaking five or six languages, lithe as a dancer, unbreasted, Gilberte, surely not the right one for Todd, too independent, that's what Elliot had told his son, she's going to hurt you, or perhaps he'd told him that he, Todd, would hurt her. What a tangle of words these marriages turned out to be. Lawyers and contracts and settlements—like brave forts perched on some river awaiting the enemy. Someone would be hurt, and someone was.

The cotton shirt, the tiny, stiff buttons, the starched edge of the shirt—was there a word for that, for the doubled strip of cloth containing the button holes? Elliot's shaking, she hadn't noticed it before, or he'd hidden it from her. Or she'd noticed and ignored it. Elliot wasn't someone to whom one paid attention. Death began in just the way that love begins—with a simple sign that you mis-read. A trembling limb on a sunny afternoon, at the moment you'd be least prepared to notice. "*Ahi come,/Come passata sei,/Cara compagna dell'eta mia nova.*" To be honest, Elle thought, not the dear companion of my innocence since there'd been little innocence when we met. And what was innocence in those days? Ignorance, she supposed. *Nocere.* Not harming. But she'd done much harm, nothing crim-inal, but still, harm, hurting. The aspirant upfront. A voiceless pharyngeal fricative, if she remembered correctly. *Unamuno.* Miguel de. She had to look up that name. Not a natural poet herself, Elle couldn't think of what she wanted to express about the moment she'd met Elliot or the years during which she'd lost him, or what she would say about all the moments in between. Something in pentameter. "I cried at the loss of love I lacked." She had paper and pen in her pocket and wrote the line down just in case, and the words "shirt front" and *Unamuno,* underlined twice. Elliot had been good to her but bad for her, and the prepositions mattered—he'd treated her well, but ruined her life. Or she had ruined his and this in turn had ruined hers. *Toward death inclines even the rules of love.* "Ruined my life," when spoken aloud sounded not only false but dishonest, self-pitying. "No he didn't." The line was wrong and had to be fixed. Not "rules," for love has none. Maybe "practice" since the thing was always more an art than a science, the giving of oneself to another, or to one's children—she hadn't done that, hadn't been inclined toward self-abrogation for poor Todd, *Tod*, her life's error, not the child, but her own unbending heart—unyielding. "I am unyielding," Elle spoke to the ravens mingled with crows that were coaxing sunflower seeds from the feeder she'd put up for the finches. *Fra poco in me quell'ultimo/Dolore anco fu spento.* Elle smiles at this idea. No, the pain never dies, but *dolore* is so lovely, *dolorosa*, she can't resist jotting this on the paper as well. The thought of Simon offering to carry the cross made her weep even now. Can you imagine it? No one holds a chair for you any longer, but this man took the cross. She had stood once in the courtyard of the Church of the Holy Sepulchre, walked the Via Dolorosa, imagined the procession to Golgotha, or tried to—at certain times the mind simply shuts down, focuses on the trivial rather than on what is, in truth, too momentous to imagine. At Auschwitz it was the same thing; standing in Birkenau she had closed her eyes with the secular reverence required—no tears would come, though she had wanted, upon entering beneath the notorious gate—"*Arbeit macht frei*"—to summon tears, to faint under the weight of history's cruelty, instead she couldn't shake the chilling lines from Dante, "Through me you pass into the City of woe/Through me you pass into eternal pain," nor could she resist imagining the Florentine poet and his guide crossing to Dis, even while silently reciting the verses to herself, intoning them like a prayer. Elle felt guilty and somehow unhinged—how could she let herself be so distracted? Must she be dithering with poems even here? And then, within the walls of the crematorium, she offered a prayer for the dead, Kaddish, but it was no good, the images of gas and fire, the smell of death, the cries of the dying, all leaked away in the dusty light that struck the floor, the odor of dirt and cement, the weight of her living body on a blazing hot day. Sufficient reverence, Elle thought, was impossible. All she had at her disposal were gestures. She crossed herself—when had she last done that—and hoped that would suffice. *Dolorosa.*

No finches this year, only the noisy carrion eaters, plump and thick-billed. Indigo-feathered. Right next to violet on the double rainbows that wouldn't show up until late April when the first waves of heat lifted from El Paso toward Estancia. Silky violet, intelligent birds, sociable squabbles that reminded Elle of car trips, of her mother and father kvetching over where to stop for lunch, her father drawn to burger joints and pizza, her mother unwilling to lower her gustatory standards, even if the highway presented few options beyond McDonald's. Elle had gone around gathering the ravens' molted feathers, thinking of making some kind of display—a stupid idea—but winter days bore down and needed filling. Molting. *Ecdysis*. In her serviceable Greek: *ekdusis*, shedding something, which was what life came to be in one's seventh decade—shedding what had worn out, old skin, rotted teeth, husbands and children and friends. You began naked and ended that way, having taken on and thrown off a lifetime's worth of debris. The snow covered the yard and trees and didn't melt but molted the landscape that emerged as fresh as when her dermatologist burned away the moles on her back. The clean skin of desert that surrounded her. She adored Cornell boxes and might after all make something of her worn bits of flotsam. Or was it jetsam? She'd look later on, but she knew that she'd forget at once. Some things eluded every effort—

memorizing poems by Robert Frost, recalling how much powdered sugar to put in her icing recipe, the precise date of her son's birth. Perhaps flotsam floats and jetsam flies. Or one is lost at sea and one is jettisoned. Junk in any case, debris, such as lined the roads around Estancia, beer cans appearing on Sunday mornings picked up by DUI crews attired in orange only to be re-tossed and picked up, Elle imagined, by some of the tossers themselves. *Tossers*: perfect. One morning she'd found an entire case of Budweiser empties dumped in her driveway—the Saturday after Thanksgiving—bottles, some of them shattered, spilling out of a Smith's bag embossed with a garish red turkey. She'd been more amused than angry—what did she expect? With so much land lying about, fields shorn of grass by generations of cattle and sheep, stunted piñon trees half dead in the drought, berms of brown sand spilling onto the highway in the heavy winds, why bother with disposal? Like the thousands of useless satellites and booster rockets floating above earth, the junkyard of human aspiration, the cost of yearning for the stars, aluminum and titanium and God knows what else that all came hurtling to earth, landing, mostly, in the sea. Flotsam or jetsam.

⁓

Her neighborhood. To have landed here at last. Among the drinkers and ranchers and ravens. Handsome birds. Todd had gone unloved and survived. There was a lesson in that. Too much, Elle thought as she went ahead and refilled her cup for a third time (against the rules!), too much noise about love. As if it were oxygen. She was in a hard mood this morning, flinty as the light, the mood she would have to be in to work. The mood she liked best—taking no prisoners. The work required that she be uncompromising—her cruelty was a ploy, a trick she used to obliterate her feelings so that she could feel his feelings. A vessel. It wasn't mystical, it was a matter of being open to someone else's words, whatever that meant. Elle dumped her new, untasted cup down the drain, but she didn't stir from her outpost at the window—she wiped at the panes and wondered how, even when in possession of the fullest possible knowledge of the mechanism whereby hot and cold and humid produce condensation on a window, she could no more comprehend the moisture on the glass than the astonishing fact of the tears in her eyes. Age had caused her feelings to become untrustworthy—they bubbled up in unexpected ways—she ran hot and cold, hard

as stone one minute and weeping the next—
absurd. The body was undependable enough, but
to lose control of one's feelings was insupportable.
Remember menopause? Twenty years before, a
breather between living and beginning the long
slide toward death. Not unlike the top of the Ferris
wheel, that frightening split second between rising
and falling. A flood of memories bubbled up. Not
iron, but George Ferris (Elle knew it was George
but checked out of habit—the old Britannica was
right there in the kitchen, where Mrs. Housewife
would have Fanny Farmer and James Beard she
stored the eleventh edition), 1893, the World's Fair
or Exposition—the World's Unfair, oh she liked
that, the Expo being a testimony to what the Chicago working classes could never hope to possess,
and wasn't that the point, to keep the boundar-
ies clear? George Ferris. "George" was Elle's least
favorite male name, stinking of madness. George
II, George Apley. George Babbitt. *Fer* as in bring-
ing fertility and suffering; bearing the unbearable.
What had it been like, sitting atop the iron con-
traption, looking over the Exposition? The crowd
seen for the first time from above and not from
within. Her first time, at nine, rewarded with a
day at Coney Island for earning gold stars on her

report card. Third grade, she thought, and never had the world seemed so frightening as from fifty feet up. She choked up her hot dog, her biliousness caused by the realization—it hadn't occurred to her before—that she was indistinguishable from everyone else.

The sun was up and she had to go to work. Her ambition was a tide that pulled her in one direction only. Filling blank pages with someone else's words, with her version of someone else's words. All day and many nights she played with sound and meaning, with diction and syntax, imagined a reader casting her eyes on the words she, Elle, had conjured from her poet. Sibyl. Naturally Elle and Elliot had joined a busload of tourists in scrambling up the duty hill at Delphi. Some kind of gas leaked from the broken rock, or so she'd read. The view had been worth the climb, and for a few moments Elle had understood the meaning of mystery, the notion of *mystes*, of being selected for something difficult yet important. What were poems but mysteries? The best ones, his for example, never yielded their secrets, they were, like prophecies, oblique and confounding. They took time and, in the end—Elle felt sure of this—they came as a gift from the gods.

Nonetheless, she dawdled. There was a place nagging at her, not a mountaintop, not broiling Greece (it had been July when they went, a "jaunt" as Elliot styled it, a reward for a promotion; in any case, the heat had been unbearable), but someplace in mid-winter, just like now. Leopardi had written a poem that she could recite without thinking, but didn't just then, instead she said aloud, "My mind sinks in this immensity," a lovely line, one she'd found yesterday, making something of "*Immensita s'annega il pensier mio*," deciding to put the mind first and immensity last. Immensity sinks the mind. Now she had it. When she was ten, Elle had been sent to live with her grandmother, the German one. She had been put on the third floor, in the garret—a cubbyhole in the attic—and at night she would crawl out of bed to peer at the stars through the tiny window whose purpose wasn't vision but ventilation. It was here that she had first felt immensity, the word itself opening to the fact of distance. She had sat at her grandmother's kitchen table, before the stained stove on which potatoes boiled and sausage fried, sat quietly while her grandmother, innocent of Elle's presence, spoke German to the bubbling pots. Sat, and with a bit of pencil, wrote out light years, strings of zeros marking the distance to Orion's belt. Seven-hundred light years. Six trillion miles, the zeros flowing across the page like a string of insects. She counted the stars, named the brighter ones after her literary heroes (Pippi and Anne), attempted to see the constellations—a bull, a winged horse, twins. All she saw were random points of light that appeared to be just out of reach, no further away than a ship at sea glimpsed from her grandmother's front porch. The house, a rambling, three-story Victorian, was on Beach Street, half a block from the boardwalk, the ocean clearly visible except on those days when fog filled the narrow strip of land between the sea and the bay, billows of smoky salt air that dampened sound. She could see the twilit sun behind the fog, the disconcerting feeling of neither day nor night. The memory was vivid enough to make her catch her breath. In such a fog one could see anything.

Elle sat down hard at the kitchen table. Her heart was beating too quickly. She folded her hands in her lap. "Oh Lord," she began, but that was all she had to say. Elle had given up sending prayers into the void. She might chant something more *a la mode,* words in a Buddhist or Taoist vein, paradoxes, the sort of thing God appeared to prefer. "Oh Lord," and then "Do no harm," "Let me work today," modest prayers offered to the god-man serenely seated beneath the sheltering Bodhi tree—the incarnation of irony. Her prayer flags and incense basket above the mineral-stained porcelain toilet, and the altar next to her bed— the church of Elle. The altar purchased for her by Todd on one of his periodic business excursions to Asian countries where he could exploit the cheap labor and thereby pad his own nest-- *E via se li reca al diletto/suo nido*—that nest as well, and his latest, his Taiwanese bride, Miss Lucing, Loosing, rescued from one of his factories, a story not unlike Puccini's, teak and ivory—cheap in lesser China—with the tiny Buddha figure perched upon a delicate silk cushion, sewn, Elle knew, by a child whose fingers could handle the stitches. She would have thrown it out years before but Todd always asked about it, "the triptych," which it wasn't, but what does a corporate accountant know of such matters? So there it was, her flags and incense and wooden icon and occasional vague prayers offered in lieu of getting to work. But Elle believed—how could she not?

—◆◆◆—

When Elle had agreed to do Leopardi a decade before—the *Canti*—she'd had no idea what she faced. It wasn't the language, or at least not only the language. She'd done Cavalcanti and Ungaretti, and won the Bollingen for her Umberto Saba when she was thirty-six—her best work she thought, lyrics she could still recite after a five-year struggle with the great bookseller, *O nell'antica carne dell'uomo troppo addentro infitta antica brama*….a line she had translated (she remembered exactly) without the interjection, thinking it antiquated: *The ancient flesh of man buried deep within his ancient desire*—not quite correct of course, the desire being general and not belonging to any "him"—desire buried deep within—or the flesh of man with its deep desires. None of these versions was literal, but Elle had never been a literal translator, preferring to recapture the "spirit of the poet." which is how she put it to her agent, Barbara Gelbert. "I channel the work," the phrase she'd uttered to Barbara in some posh Manhattan eatery still made Elle cringe, making herself out as a medium for a man of whose life she knew nothing. What are poems but departures from ordinary living, ways of stopping time, arresting age, thwarting death? "Channeling the poet," as if she were a box full of tubes and transistors catching signals from Rome or Florence and putting them into tidy boxes of English that she happened to have handy. Not the man, but the poem, putting herself, as she said in interviews, "Within the words themselves," which wasn't possible and she knew it, but it was a noble ideal for a translator—not simply to move words from one language into another, but to live with the originals for years and then, though some alchemy no one understood, bring them back to life in English. *Ha fatto un sogno*—it was a dream, this falling into language. Elle had told her publisher that a fixed deadline wasn't possible since she had no idea how long she would have to live with Saba in order to make her own versions. Fine, he had told her, than you will have to live with him without an advance. And she had. She'd gone to work for Neil Harris, editing science textbooks—a relaxing break from Saba given how pedestrian the books had been, how dull. Elle had known Harris in college and was allowed to come and go as she saw fit, to work at home, to take sabbaticals for her translation work. So they'd lived on

Elliot's resident's salary and the gifts his Episcopalian parents had bestowed—generous gifts, and not unwelcome. And then Elliot had finished up and after another decade they'd left Boston and moved to Washington—to Bethesda. Elliot had started working at George Washington and there was plenty of money—too much—but Elle stuck with the textbooks to have an excuse to leave the house. An excuse to get away from work she loved but which took a toll. Slowly the Saba had come together and sold reasonably well and won the Bollingen, and then, years later, after working on an anthology of contemporary Italian poetry and a novel by Laura di Falco, trying and failing with Dante's *Vita Nuova,* collaborating on a prose *Purgatorio,* publishing her own poems to no acclaim and no sales, then, God help her, a contract to do Leopardi. A selection only, a few lyrics. Two years of work. But in the midst of the selection there was an escalation, a call for the *Canti,* a more difficult undertaking. How difficult she hadn't known at the time. "One never does know," she said now. (It wasn't madness to speak aloud now and then; she was alone, and there were times when hearing one's own voice was a comfort.) "The finest poems ever written," and she believed that they were, the finest and most difficult to make her own. The poet whose words were his and no one else's. But she wanted to try them, to see if she was up to it. That was ten years ago. A decade she'd lived with Leopardi, "the greatest genius of Italian literature," she'd told her publisher, hoping to be forgiven the years of delay in producing her versions of poems that she now thought were untranslatable. Or appeared to be so—a thought which raised a question that Elle preferred not to consider. Had she been wasting her life?

"Buried deep within his ancient desire." What in the world did that line mean? What about desire was ancient? To be buried—to bury oneself. "He had buried himself in desire that was ancient." Well, that wasn't poetry. Buried in ancient desire…. Aren't we all? Every word mattered, every nuance. Something of the mystical in the whole business, as in finding oneself disembodied, awash in a realm of language. The names of things, either arbitrary and without attachment to the world—sounds made with the equipment of the mouth or lines drawn on paper--or somehow natural, as Plato believed. On this single point, Elle was a resolute Platonist. Words were real, eternal, and could not be separated from the things to which they were attached. The proof was in poetry, a way of being and not only of writing. She was overthinking Leopardi's words, but she knew his beliefs were her own. She lingered over each word, inviting distraction, avoiding finishing—pushing away completion— her own, she supposed, as much as his. Age did that—you couldn't rush just when the urgency to do so was greatest. She no longer channeled but exchanged—the work made her feel as if she were a banker, turning Euros to dollars or Yuan to Pounds Sterling. What would people feel as they read these versions of hers? Would they weep or laugh, or throw the book against the wall? For the first time in forty years she had no idea of how to proceed. "He's eluded me," Elle said, as if Leopardi were a lover who had thrown her over for someone else. As she sat at her ancient kitchen table, the light now bright enough to illuminate the *ristras* outside the window, Elle regretted the loss of her ability to see the words rightly, to feel what they meant. "I've been solving puzzles," she thought, which struck the right note of self-pity. She'd been preparing herself for the *Canti* her entire life, living with them in Washington for years, and now, her husband dead, she was alone with the maddening tubercular romantic in the desolation of rural New Mexico. Of all the places she might be, had been, had dreamed of visiting or of settling into for the final years of her life, of all the visions she had had, dreams of beach-front cottages or city apartments, she now found herself alone in a hundred-year-old rambling wooden house in a dying town on the edge of a plain whose extent she couldn't even imagine. What was it? *Sannyasa* or *Vanaprastha*—one was a hermit, the other a wandering monk. No more wandering on these legs. In a state that most Americans apparently couldn't locate on a map, where the governor had to affirm that English was understood, where, according to the demographics published in the *Journal*, old white ladies like her were few and far between.

"I'm going mad," she said, though Elle didn't believe in madness, at least not for persons like herself, a woman with work to do isn't the sort to go crazy. But if she were mad her sins would be forgiven—she could give up working and move to a retirement home. "Mute Mews" or "Terminal Apartments." *Sin* was a fine word: missing the mark, a bad toss of the spear. "My sins," Elle summed up, a mini-biography, an epitaph, "were lapses in what is a fundamentally sound character." I'm eccentric, not odd. Elle couldn't bear to be odd; more than fame as a poet she'd wished to be normal, unlike her mother who was distinctly *odd*. She was nothing more or less than a widow living in a dusty village of boarded-up shops, one cafe, two bars, and the agricultural coop. She drove to Moriarty for groceries and gas. A woman living alone, content, toting up her days, scurrying about among dictionaries and memories. A harmless enough existence. Elle knew half-a-dozen women in Estancia who had lost their husbands, rancher's wives whose men had fallen off horses or fallen under tractors, men who had put on too much weight and died while watching television. She might have ended up stuck in a double-wide with only Social Security, satellite TV, and a feral dog between her and suicide. But she didn't, thanks to her education, upbringing, and—to be honest—her neurotic personality. Always a workaholic, dutiful, unable to bear the slightest criticism, the brightest girl in class, the one with the neatest penmanship, the best speller, the girl who attended summer classes for edification rather than for remediation. "A little toady," Elle thought, a teacher's pet, but so what? Better to *invest one-self*, as her father loved to say, *invest yourself* in everything that you do. Her father had been big on commitment, though only for other people. He remained, as far as Elle could tell, uninvested in everything—in his wife and daughter, in his job, in friendships—the few he'd allowed himself—in his beliefs, if he'd had any. "Your father," Cristina had confided to Elle when she was old enough to know the truth, "your father enjoys being unattached to anything, including, I'm afraid, to us." Elle had taken this news amicably, having at the time no idea what her mother was talking about. *Daddy*, a slender pale handsome man, well-dressed, close-shaven, smelling of limes, a presence in the house when he was home, an absence when he was not, a godlike figure in whom she believed absolutely, believed in precisely (she later understood) as a girl of a certain age believes in horses or field hockey or boys, and this blind, unquestioning belief, as Elle came to understand it, was actually a confession of ignorance. She'd blamed her mother for her father's departure, but when she was honest with herself—not often enough—it was her father who was the ghost, and her unyielding mother who had been her life's substance.

Elle had been thinking of stopping. Throwing

Leopardi over once and for all—she'd done it before. Years ago, when she'd finished the first ten poems she'd sent them to her friend Gioia Solara at Columbia. What did she think? Had they any value as poetry, were they at all close to Leopardi's originals? Solara's report had been discouraging. She felt many of the lines fell flat, or missed the nuances of the original. "They lack subtlety," her friend had written, and Elle feared she was right. "*Ultimo canto di Saffo*," one of Elle's favorite poems, had taken her weeks; she had thought her version strong and original. "It's no good," Solara had called Elle, not wanting to express herself in her "poor English"—Gioia's English was perfect—in a letter, "'*Qual fallo mai, qual si nefando eccesso…*' the lines beginning here, some of Leopardi's most exquisite verses," Gioia thought that Elle had gotten them wrong, "the spindle of Fate," Sappho is decrying the blind power of the world, lamenting her inability to make herself, but you make her sound guilty, not angry, someone responsible rather than resigned." Elle remembered all of it. They'd argued, in Italian, over words and lines and the mysterious transformation of Sappho's voice, which no one knew apart from a handful of her poems, into Leopardi's voice and words, the alchemy of his putting his ideas into her mind. How had he done it? She was three removes from the truth, or four if you counted the Muse herself. How could Elle get at feelings of helplessness so foreign to people who believed absolutely in their agency, in their ability to live whatever life they chose? Americans hated poetry for just this reason: its intimacy was frightening to people who preferred to skim the truths of living, whatever they might be. Writing poems was like serving over-spiced food at the dinner party; the guests might pretend to taste it, but would never eat it and never return for more. Elle had been distraught by her friend's criticisms. She'd put the work aside for a year. But what would she do? When she'd started translating she hadn't understood the difficulties. At first she and Elliot had simply needed the money. Harcourt had given her a $2,000 advance for an edition of Italian poetry inspired by the events of 1848—Gioberti, Balbo, Giusti and a handful of others. The advance had come from the Italian-American Solidarity Association, $5,000 in all, and had been a godsend. Elliot had started his internship at Mass General. Elle had been staying home, looking half-heartedly for a job, hoping to get pregnant or publish a book of her own—either one would have suited her. Sitting (still!) at her kitchen table, Elle could remember mornings spent in this exact position, in this identical chair, her arms draped just so, or perhaps holding a glass of milk, hoping to build up her bones, worried that she'd begin to droop as her mother had done in her last years. Their one-bedroom apartment was in Medford, a small town where the rents were affordable. There hadn't been anything to do; Elle was alone most of the time. But she hadn't wanted company or anything to do—no shops or clubs or sports or friends. She was in her twenties, recently married, not ambitious but not indolent either. She had justified doing nothing by telling herself that she was "getting ready for the rest of her life," warming up like an athlete about to enter a game. When Elle had written to her mother to say that she was "examining her life" she meant that she wasn't thinking about occupations or babies or being the wife of a thoracic surgeon, but that she was deciding what kind of person she would become. She was considering her inner life, thinking about her "soul," a word that, back then, Elle had deliberately placed in quotation marks, as if to say, "as if." Elle took pleasure in disappointing the modest expectations of her mother—had there been a stepfather by then? She couldn't recall. Her mother was a staunch Catholic, ultramontane, regal and aloof. Without ever spending a day with her mother, having no more contact than was afforded by punctual monthly letters full of platitudes about the weather and current events, three or four holiday phone calls—birthdays and Christmas and, for some reason, Labor Day—in other words, knowing nothing whatsoever about her mother's life aside from the fact that she was selling real estate and might have remarried, Elle had decided that somehow she, Elle, was the victim of a great injustice, and that what had happened to her beloved father was—she couldn't have said how— her mother's fault. Elle knew that there aren't two sides to every story but fifty. Being angry with her mother had given Elle something to write about in her barren Medford apartment. Short stories—terrible pastiches of Alice Munro—poems--dreadful, maudlin verses modeled on Sylvia Plath, all the rage back then, and Sharon Olds, poems seething with rage—poems and stories that reprised the anger Elle felt at having had a mostly happy childhood. What greater inspiration was there than unhappiness? And if you aren't lucky enough to be unhappy, then that's reason enough to be miserable. It embarrassed Elle to remember how wrapped up she had been in grief that she had spun from her own imagination. Alone, she brooded. Elliot was gone for sixteen hours a day, and when he came home it was to collapse in exhaustion. He would stumble in the door and apologize for being late. "You're always late." Elle felt ungenerous much of the time, though she could also be tender and solicitous. She'd heat up canned soup and make her husband a cheese sandwich, but Elliot would already have passed out on the bed. Elle would pull off his shoes and pants and set the clock to allow her husband five hours of sleep, just as he had instructed her. What then? She wrote, scribbling in pencil on yellow pads, throwing almost everything out, occasionally typing up a story for *The New Yorker*, always believing that when the polite handwritten rejection arrived that it would be an effusive acceptance and a big check. She'd sold a few stories and poems to little magazines for contributors' copies and felt stupid when she showed the badly printed and poorly bound editions of *Blue Iris* and *Glissade* to her husband. Elliot would politely read her work (when it was in print, never would he read a draft) and say he *liked* the poem or found the story *interesting*, but offer nothing else. Which was fine. Elle had once or twice requested a fuller response, but Elliot would just repeat that he thought the story was "really well done" and lapse into a silence that precluded further inquiry. Since he wasn't much of a reader, Elliot didn't expect his wife to rely on his opinion, just as he never asked her to check out an article in the *Journal of Thoracic Surgery*. They lived in slightly intersecting bubbles, and once Elle understood that this was the case she decided that either she could divorce Elliot and start her life over, or she could accept the companionable arrangement they had established, and get on with her life. It was an easy decision. Elle had no desire to be on her own, and there was no way she was going to remarry. She'd liked Elliot well enough. He was kind and smart and handsome in a bland New England way. "I was the sort of girl who bought the first dress she tried on, the first pair of shoes." Elliot, she had ruefully come to understand, had been handy. He was her "type," that odd concept. He wasn't chatty, nor was he self-centered; he was a modest, hard-working, well-spoken gentleman who genuinely seemed to like her. And things, overall, had worked out. One child, financial security, shared tastes in travel and leisure, long spells of mutual silence that implied no recrimination. Yes, it had been a decent enough marriage, nothing spectacular, but whose marriage was spectacular? Workmanlike was about right. Early on, trapped in Medford, thinking about becoming a writer or some other kind of brainworker, Elle went on long walks around the dismal apartment complex, ignoring her low-rent neighbors. Some days she took their rusted VW Bug and drove to Stop and Shop or to the horrible strip mall for a movie. In the grocery store she would wander the aisles, not shopping but browsing, day-dreaming, watching the moms with their little children, women whose features were difficult to make out, lots of hair and make-up, an urgency in their trolling of the aisles. In no hurry herself, Elle would lean on her cart, pick up a loaf of wheat bread, a jar of sauerkraut, some canned corn, spend half an hour selecting an affordable wine for dinner. Elle felt peaceful squeezing cantaloupes—she hated cantaloupe—or checking the Spanish onions for soft spots. What would she cook? Borscht? Leek soup? Pound quoting Dante came to mind—"*Io venni in luogo d'ogni luce muto*;/The stench of wet coal...." Da da dum dum. Something. Addressing crowds through their arse-holes...there was more, the crowds and their sorrowful carts reminded Elle of the fecal—piles of food turned to rivers of shit. Flushed away, stirred into a brown swill and washed out to sea. Everything, Elle thought, ends up in the ocean. Not ashes to ashes: saltwater and shit were the medium of life. Pound the misanthropic Jew-baiter, his poetry full of hatred. *Odor di terra.* She had a book with her when she shopped, or when she walked or sat at the dentist's for a filling—Antonia Pozzi, not her favorite, but good enough for Medford. How odd she must have looked wandering the streets mumbling poems, sitting distracted in the Commons, sifting though a dictionary, trying to pin down the meaning of a line. Elliot wouldn't have moved when she returned from the grocery store. She would stand over him, wishing him awake so that she could hear someone's voice. If it were still daylight Elle would quietly open the bedroom blinds just enough to stir the dust motes. Elliot moved, turned away from the window, and mumbled something in a language Elle didn't understand. She would sit alone in the kitchen, at this same table, the same stain on the wood, the chip in the edge where Elliot's friend—Roger? A heavy man with a shaggy beard—dropped it during the move to Bethesda. The table was a gift from his parents. She and Elliot had eaten ten thousand meals at this table; talked about work and their child, quarreled. It was right here, across from where Elle now sat that Elliot had discussed his diagnosis—he'd live a good while longer, of that he was certain, not, unfortunately, counting on the failure of his heart. He admitted that there would be difficult days. Elle might want to bring in a nurse. No, there would be no nurses. She would cope with whatever happened. And she did, more or less.

All of these random memories sped through Elle's brain like minnows through a warm shallow, each jot of recollection a tiny fish, living for just a few seconds before gobbled by some larger, more predatory entity—the rattle of the stove as it demanded more cedar, or the rumble in her empty stomach. You couldn't stop it for even a second. Elle had tried meditating during her Mary-land days—she couldn't bring herself to pronounce the word "Maryland"—*merdelend* is how the natives said it—but the idea of "becoming empty," or of "listening to the silence within" was impossible, even perverse. No, her brain never slowed from the moment she awoke until (she supposed) the second that she dipped from thinking into full unconsciousness—a blessed moment that, frankly, Elle had come to yearn for at the end of each day, a transition one could never hope to capture no matter how hard one tried—awake, asleep, awake. Elle also noticed that she couldn't remember what position she was in when she awoke. Her marriage bed—an enormous queen-sized thing that Elliot had insisted upon—offered room enough for an entire family, but Elle confided herself to a sliver of space on the very edge, fetal and uncovered (she woke up shivering). The second she awoke it began: the cacophony of voices that she supposed belonged to her. Birdsong, tree rustle, snow slide, house creak. And off she went.

She could stop now. Elle computed carefully, as if counting gold coins. She had come to the end—to the last place she would live, the last work she would do, fading out, a song that repeated into silence. She would finish, tidy her books and papers and memories. And complete the *Canti*. No leaving this work undone. She owed it to Leopardi to bring his book into English. Her name would be forgotten, but his would never perish, at least as long as poetry mattered, which, Elle had to admit, wasn't much longer. "You can't live for contingencies," she thought. That poetry mattered was an article of faith, but she couldn't have said why. Why should poems count for more than this well-built table, or the silver she had inherited from her grandmother? The argument Elle had made for years had something to do with poetry as the highest literary form, with poems carrying consciousness from one person to another, across ages and continents. Granted, it was a vague idea, so vague that she now found herself unwilling to get back to work, back to *Il Risorgimento*, a poem that felt to Elle as if it had been addressed directly to her, a stumbling block in the *Canti* that must be overcome. She wondered if she hadn't been wasting her time, imagining importance where there was only occupation. "I'm spinning my wheels, " thought Elle, remembering the winter Sunday she and Elliot had driven to the top of Mt. Taylor and hiked for hours in what had been at first a wispy snowfall but which quickly transformed into a blizzard of dry powder. It had been ten degrees at 11,000 feet according to Elliot's thermometer. Her husband had been fond of scientific instruments and could always be relied upon to know the barometric pressure. When they finally reached their car the drifts had piled over the tires. It had taken them an hour to dig out and put on the chains and inch through the parking lot to the (luckily) long downhill road back to Grants. It had been a close call. Or so Elle had thought at the time. Elliot laughed at her panic, as he thought of it, but she knew he'd been frightened as well. "Spinning one's wheels" became an expression Elle used when she wished to convey futility. Leopardi had known about wheel spinning. "He yearned for love," Elle had written in the introduction she had promised her publisher. "He yearned for love, and to be free of his oppressive Catholic family." Elle had been drawn to Leopardi in part because of his struggle with his mother. He had grown up in a devout household—piety had nearly drowned him. Elle's mother had insisted on Mass and catechism, Saturday confession, nightly prayers, fish on Fridays, renunciations at Lent. Now, once again among the believers, in a town with a single public building—Saint Teresa's Roman Catholic Church—Elle thought of Hegel's idea that the absence of something can be more powerful, more real, than its presence. Estancia's landscape was Tuscany's—desiccated, sandy, scattered with broken granite and contorted piñon. *"Ne me diceva il cor che l'età verde/Sarei dannato a consumare in questo/Natio borgo selvaggio, intra una gente...*" Leopardi had written "*zotica*" which didn't fit her neighbors at all. Yes, she lived among poor people (not boors!) who cared nothing for knowledge—Hispanic Catholics farmers, mechanics and day laborers—but she wasn't, as Leopardi had been, wasting the springtime of her life among louts. In Estancia, she was the oddball, the loco widow who drove a beat-up pickup and lived alone in a broken-down house. Once in a while she drank a cup of tea in Buck's Café. She hired local high school boys to trim her trees and patch her roof—but she wasn't one of them. "What is freedom but solitude?" Though Leopardi had wanted to find love, Elle knew from reading the *Notebooks* that he couldn't break away from his past, from the constraints on feeling that had been placed upon him by his upbringing. Knowing this, relating to him in his loneliness, Elle thought there was a chance for her to reach the meaning of his poems.

She rose from her seat too quickly and nearly fell. Holding onto the table, she waited for the dizziness to ease before she moved to the sideboard. There was a fresh loaf of bread and she cut a slice, buttered it, and walked back into the living room to stoke the fire. It was full light, though no warmer. Elle slipped on her heavy cardigan, her "writing sweater" as Elliot had called it—"Ah, I see you're in your writing sweater. I'd better take a walk"—and he'd disappear for hours, spending them, Elle knew, not walking but sitting on a bench in the Commons. This was in their post-Medford days when Elliot, done with his residency, was working fifty-hour weeks, and on the occasions when he was home he'd be eager to get away, to be alone for a while, unstressed. He'd loved surgery, but it took a toll. Everyone, he told his wife, cuts something. "We've been doing it since the Greeks," and he'd spin out his theory of how the ancients had discovered a way to cover up their ignorance by chopping every fact and idea up into smaller pieces, "until the tiny bits could no longer be thought of as anything but spirits, and spirits aren't amenable to further chopping. They're the end of the line. And so you think you know something when you get to them, something important—the essence of the world—but really all you've done is a lot of chopping." Elle listened to this lecture often, and never asked Elliot what he was talking about. He was, Elle thought (sometimes lovingly, sometimes impatiently) pedantic for a manual laborer. What else was a surgeon but a well-compensated craftsman? He went to work and cut people open, fiddled with their lungs and put them back together—more or less. She was a snob when it came to her husband. Though he'd gone to Tufts and served an internship and a residency at one of the finest hospitals in the country and practiced his craft for twenty-five years, she couldn't work up much enthusiasm for medicine. What mattered were words. It was an odd notion—why not birds or gourmet food or Renaissance paintings? Or saving people's lives, as Elliot doubtlessly did? These things did matter, but only when experienced at second hand, through language. Not birds, but books about them; not elaborate meals and dealing with waiters and sommeliers but books by M.F.K. Fisher. Not treks to Italy to pass days in the Uffizi looking at paintings, but novels or, better, poems, about the experience of wandering the galleries of the Uffizi—the scent of linseed oil and the dusty light captured in Italian. Just so she didn't have to rouse herself and make a trip, or leave the world of language behind in order to have first-hand experiences that were just as good—better—when enjoyed vicariously. It was too much, all these possibilities. Where would you go, and how would you get there? Where would you stay and how much would it cost and would the food be good and how homesick would you feel? There wasn't enough time for ordinary life, and Elle disliked the waste of time above all else, even if, in not "cavorting about" she didn't do anything but sit in her living room and stare out the window. She still walked most afternoons—she'd once been a great walker, a Dorothy Wordsworth walker—but now she ambled in the vicinity of her ramshackle house, especially since she'd been bitten by one of her neighbors' dogs, a pit bull, and was transported by ambulance to Albuquerque for treatment. The walks weren't the pleasure they had once been, the pleasure drained from them by a thoughtless neighbor, which was the way all pleasures were taken away—by the thoughtless.

And yet, travel had been a big part of her life, of her life with Elliot, especially when he cut back on work. There was money enough for cruises, but the thought of a cruise was unsupportable—trapped on a ship of fools—so twice each year they had flown to a European city, never to Asia or South America—too foreign for Elliot—and spent a week eating and visiting tourist attractions. Neither of them had especially enjoyed these trips—there were good restaurants and plenty of tourist attractions in Washington—but traveling was something that well-heeled Americans simply had to do. It said so in the *Times*. Week after week they read articles about Budapest and Sofia, about the memorable meals reporters on expense accounts had enjoyed in Copenhagen, and it seemed almost irresponsible not to decamp from their too large home and fly (first-class!) to a city where, sure enough, the food was elegant and the hotels were four stars. And yet there was something not quite right about it, not quite comforting about wandering around in a city full of strangers who were at home, going about their business, living where, in fact, they lived. Elle had read Henry James in those days, lugging his prissy stories of expatriate Americans around like bricks of hashish (hallucinatory prose cut off in small chunks). Middle-class Americans fit nowhere. In America they imagined themselves sophisticated; in Europe, they were rubes. James wasn't the first colonial, and hardly the last, to yearn to be a good Englishman. Sitting at home in St. James, waited upon, sipping his tea, flatulent and dyspeptic, James did get one thing right: Americans, with no culture of their own, had patched together an identity that was equal parts urbane and tawdry. Not a charitable thought, but Elle's sojourns abroad, her rambles with Elliot in Paris and Rome, had convinced her that the world would be better off if her countrymen remained at home. One benefit of her old age was an excuse to stay put.

An outsider. Loco. But still, she fit nicely into the village of Estancia, population 479. On the two annual occasions when Elle mingled with her fellow Estancians—the Fourth of July and Christmas Eve—she felt nothing but affection for the single moms, retired stone cutters, part-time bean farmers, small-time cattle-ranchers, ex-hippies, and assorted day-laborers who came for ice cream and draft beer on the Fourth and for rum punch and caroling on Christmas Eve. Otherwise Elle seldom saw anyone. She'd had a lifetime's worth of socializing in Boston and Washington, following Elliot to medical school and then, when he was famous or at least a respectable figure in the medical profession—when he'd paid his dues and been noticed by Boston-area Democrats and had his name mentioned to someone who mentioned it someone else who thought of Elliot when it was time to nominate a competent if bland practicing surgeon to become under-assistant to the Deputy Director of

the National Institute of Health, going to live in a
nice house in Bethesda, a house in which she had
given parties for NIH types, for politicians, secre-
taries of this and that, uninteresting men and their
wives who all seemed to have gone to the same
colleges and pledged the same sororities and had
the same thoughts as one another, and once, mem-
orably, Elle had prepared a "nice dinner" for the
Secretary of HEW and his wife and tried to think
of something to say about national health insur-
ance but had come up short and overcooked the
risotto to boot. And she had raised a child and
made a life in a place that seemed oddly no place at
all, the epitome of American blandness in the 80's,
the years of Reagan and Bush the First, in a city
where war and peace had about the same meaning,
where you wore a black dress and heels five nights
a week and sipped watery drinks and ate bad food
and pretended to be fascinated by people whose
interests were not your own, whose interests were
not even *their* own. It had been her time in the wil-
derness. She'd been miserable, but docile, a wife
and mother and hostess, infiltrating a world that
meant nothing to her.

As the thought crossed her mind—"I could

have lived my life as I wished"—Elle smiled. She hadn't a spontaneous bone in body. Everything she'd ever done she'd planned out—all the large life-changing things to be sure, but even the minutiae. Elliot had called her "the engineer," and she'd taken this as a compliment. Not an engineer any longer, she thought as she lingered, first at the window—the juncos had reclaimed the feeder from the crows, little birds dressed in tuxedos, "the hurl and gliding/rebuffed the big wind"—then back at the kitchen table where the line from Hopkins materialized as if from the splintering oak surface itself. In the end, what could you control? Hadn't her sitting here well after seven in the morning—so late—been foreordained? Elle recalled the shock she had felt when she'd first seen a graphic depiction of the human gene, the Rosetta stone of every human life, "a hieroglyph," she said, and then she jotted the words "What language is DNA?" meaning, she supposed, how would one characterize the syntax of evolution? A, T, C, G. Elliot had explained the "*ines*" to her, but she'd have to unbox one of his biology books to remember their names. Twenty-six letters, four protein chains. Three-protein words. How many trillion cells? Both consciousness and the means to express consciousness: all elegantly and simply shaped. If God existed, then he was an artist, at least at the genetic level. Perhaps God was a novelist—history was His *War and Peace*, or *Remembrance of Things Past*. But why assume a maker? Perhaps the world is eternal. No beginning and no end. Why not? Was it reasonable to believe that all of this had been made, fashioned from matter, conjured into being by the Word? The eternity of the world had been a touchy subject in the Catholic Church, nonetheless Leopardi had written somewhere in its defense. He'd been only a half-hearted believer, or at least too independent to accept any dogma without testing it against his own intelligence. Elle rose to get the *Zibaldone* to see what he had written. And pain swept over her like an electric shock.

She would sit still for a moment. Neurons buzzing in the aftershock, Elle conjured up a few lines of poetry, this time in French. "*La lune s'attristait.*" It was fortunate that she had given up French poetry. She'd loved Mallarmé in college—but in her old age sad moons and weeping tides were silly. Why invest the world with meaning that it cannot bear? Todd's view, repeated *ad nauseam*, went roughly like this: "Everyone is the same where it matters most." "Where?" Elle would look quizzically at her son, a strange being whose existence perplexed her—"I mean we all want the same things," was his elegant way of repeating himself. Why, Elle wondered, had she bred and raised a son with so little imagination? There were few things more tedious, Elle thought, than listening to Todd expound his so-called worldview. He'd read one book in his life—she couldn't bear to name the title even to herself—and from it he'd imbibed a load of nonsense about "human nature" and "the virtue of selfishness." The "things" we allegedly all want are the stuff of millennial American happiness. Elle supposed that she and Elliot, with their odd notions about possessions and security, were to blame for turning Todd into an insecure collector of Audis and women, fine wines and profitable subsidiaries. *We turn against the past*, Elle thought, as if doing so were necessary for the arrival of the present. But this was a mistake. Nostalgia: *algos* for *nostos*, the pain we feel for our home. Not only a place, but a set of ideas that make life worth living. At her age—at last!—she'd learned the art of renunciation. But not of everything, not of the contents of her memory. Elle needed no dictionary for "nostalgia." She hadn't gone far with Leopardi before seeing it was at the heart of his poetry. His home had been a prison, so his nostalgia had to be for something else. "*I did not die and did not remain alive.*" That was it wasn't it? He was trapped between living and dying, yearning neither for life nor death—his freedom a passionate indifference. Elle pulled her paper from her pocket and saw that there was no space left to write, so she reluctantly slipped back into her horseshoes and took the plunge. No pain. So she left the kitchen, dropped another log into the large stove, and made her way to her study.

Illusions must not be condemned; they are what make the world's beauty possible. Elliot had his own illusions about the mystical nature of healing. The body wasn't a machine but interconnected systems, organic and complex but amenable to both its own and another's reason. The formulation and expounding of Elliot's quasi-mystic view of medicine—Paracelsus meets Albert Schweitzer—had seemed to Elle a form of derangement. Elliot had worked tirelessly on a collection of essays he called Notes of a Healer: Western Medicine in a Holistic Setting, a project that consumed him as he grew older and spent less time at work and became instead a kind of *eminence grise*, opining on public radio about the humane dimensions of a medical practice that seemed to most people heartless, invasive, and over-priced. Elle had worried about her husband's zealous espousal of herbal medicines and yoga in place of the therapies he had spent twenty-five years prescribing—surgery, drugs, and the diet *du jour*. What had happened? Elle knew that her husband felt he had lost his touch, had "failed" two or three patients in a short period, had been shaken and, for a time, depressed. It was unbearable for Elliot to be wrong—so he backed away from what he had been and fashioned a new Elliot, an amalgam of scientist and guru, a critic of the rationality he had once espoused. Elle hadn't understood how high the stakes were for her husband, how deeply entwined his identity as a surgeon was with his identity as a person. She was now willing to concede her blindness. After all, wasn't her life inextricably bound to words? How could she have been surprised by her husband's despair at having "killed an innocent woman" after a routine lobectomy went wrong? Elliot had patients die on him before, but he never felt responsible, never felt as if he "could have done more." Elle thought this was true of everyone all of the time, and that this particular patient's dying would be subsumed into the deaths that her husband contended with each day. But this time had been different, one death too many had unnerved Elliot, or confirmed what he persuaded himself was true—that he could no longer perform. "I'm like an athlete who has lost his edge; I don't believe in it"—the "it" being not only medicine, but reason itself. And that had been that. He'd given up surgery and devoted himself, full-time, to administration. And because he'd had little to do at NIH, he could spend his time "gathering materials," mimicking his wife in her packrat ways, preparing to write his own book. After a tedious day of meetings and memos, he began researching the history of medicine. His studies, which began simply enough with mainstream works by reputable scholars, eventually moved to murkier ground, as Elliot became fascinated by holistic, occult, and "natural" cures for diseases typically treated with drugs and surgery. While Elie translated Italian poetry, Elliot read the collected works of Rudolf Steiner and Madame Blavatsky. Sitting in separate rooms after a silent dinner, each of them sought to wrest meaning from intractable things—from the body and the soul. Elle sat in her room and imagined her husband in his—ten feet and ten miles apart. When they met in the kitchen over tea or a glass of wine they talked politics and music, but nothing serious. Elliot was unhappy—he missed the intensity of doctoring, and she felt the weight of his melancholy. They brushed past one another in those years, not strangers, but inured to one another's concerns. Nothing, Elle thought in those days, is lonelier than marriage.

An ache in her back—not unusual, but intense. Thinking how age changed the way you saw the past: since it meant more, was more alive than the present, you sentimentalized what had happened, grew harsher on the subject of your failures—and other's failures. To remember in the vague way that we remember was to reduce life to the rudiments of feeling. And the rudiments had nothing whatever to do with reality. Here was where poetry became dangerous, as dangerous as religion—the temptation to mistake fragments for wholes, words for meaning, memories for truth. Suitably forewarned, Elle now felt like she could begin work.

When Elle was a freshman in college she had drawn a roommate from one of the Chicago suburbs, a devout Catholic. At the moment she thought of the girl—she had curly red hair and a face mottled with freckles—Elle was reaching for a book, still not quite ready to settle down. As far as Elle was concerned, postponement was an art. She never began anything without putting it off. You have to be certain that you are ready, she would say, and if you're not, the work will be ruined anyway, and that time will have been wasted, so it's better to waste time in advance. Marsha Reilly. The book Elle now held was not by Leopardi but Machado, the poem to *Unamuno*, the one she had thought of a few minutes ago. Not Marsha. Could you run a house on poetry, move from room to room searching for just the right words, the poet whose sentiments mimicked your own? Mattie O'Rourke wasn't right either, but what did it matter? Her father and mother had built a mini-Vatican on a large plot of suburban land. The only secular basilica Elle had ever seen. St. Peter's of Peoria. A plaster pieta tucked in the foyer of the cruciform house whose planking was painted a blue-gray that was to have the sheen of faded granite and marble but looked instead like a beach house, worn to the color of Lake Michigan. Fourteen children aged twenty to newborn, two with Down syndrome, and two sets of twins. Elle thought the house smelled like an orchard in November, as it might have, given the piles of clothes and dishes that lay on every surface—everything decomposing. How many daily joules or watts would it take to hold together such a household? Elle, scanning Machado's Spanish and remembering Leopardi's discussion of the flaws of that language, could visualize Mrs. O'Rourke setting the table for sixteen, using paper plates and paper cups, arranging three one-gallon containers of milk at regular intervals, unpacking two large loaves of spongy white bread, ladling out a half-dozen bowls of potatoes and peas, while Dr. O'Rourke, red-haired and freckled himself, sliced a ham for what Mattie had called the *posse*. *El alma desalmada*. Leopardi would mention that "alma" had the sound of wings about it, as if Gabriel were fluttering around the room. Imagine the musculature below the white robe. The O'Rourkes left the United States for Ireland right after Roe. "We can't live there anymore, not with all the dead babies," Mattie had written to Elle from Cork. The stamp had been lovely. Elle had been snowbound with the O'Rourke's for three days over Thanksgiving. She'd been given a bed in the upstairs barracks— among the girls—six or seven female O'Rourkes, each in a virginal nightdress, stacked on bunk beds, all on their backs, no snoring, no rustling about after the Doctor had come to the door and said a prayer over them, extending his arm in a blessing that seemed blasphemous, as if he were a bishop. "Rest in peace." Mrs. O'Rouke tearing pages out of the family's collection of Catholic theology, Catholic novelists, Graham Greene and Mary McCarthy, heavily redacted, a smattering of classics. There had been a collected Keats, one of Elle's favorite poets in college, but "Le Belle Dame Sans Merci" had been excised entirely, only the stubs of the offending quire left. It might have been "willing disbelief" that condemned Keats to the fireplace (Elle imagined) in the enormous living room—how did that business about suspended disbelief go? Elle didn't feel up to investigating Keats' poetics, or were they Coleridge's, or maybe she was imagining the phrase altogether. Her memory was serviceable, but not papal. The house had shaken in the snowstorm. Low pressure over the Great Lakes held moisture in place, sucking in cold air, and, it went without saying, bitter winds from the prairie on whose extremity the O'Rourkes had built their Zion. After three days of reading censored books and eating white bread, Elle felt overjoyed when the sun broke though the muck of clouds and warmed the earth just enough to allow her to get a cab to the train station and escape back East. A week later, back at school, her roommate had told Elle how much her visit had meant to the family, how the younger girls had liked her, "They admired your calmness," and Elle, who thought she had behaved badly, was ashamed of herself. She hadn't understood anything—that much was clear. In the end it isn't the existence of illusions that should concern us but their source. What does a look or a gesture portend? Language, actions, sensations—all mislead us.

Qui passo gli anni, abbandonato, occulto,/ Senz'amor, senza vita; ed aspro a forza/Tra lo stuol de'malevoli divengo…. —I have passed years here, alone, shut in darkness, without love, without a life, and, resisting all my desires, I have inclined toward those who wish me ill—she had blocked in a rough reading of the line—a complaint against his neighbors who saw in Leopardi the arrogance of the intellectual. As here: kill the messenger. Eggheads—McNamara had been a whiz kid at Rand, neocons were churned out of Yale and Harvard and Princeton along with the geniuses that ran Wall Street. Then again what was she, or Elliot? Elle wondered if the poet had been flattered by the low opinion of the *gente zotica*, or if their resentment didn't fuel Leopardi's natural desire for solitude. She had much in common with the poet on this point—she too felt her isolation two-edged, both frightening and bracing. The headline in today's local paper was of yet another round of national elections, still months away, with bland candidates obscenely funded by those for whom they would, in due time, sell off another piece of the country's history, landscape, or character. Elle took the papers, but only skimmed the headlines—they burned well, and she liked the puzzles. When she and Elliot had lived in Washington she had attempted to inoculate herself against the tedium and immorality of the political world that surrounded her. It was impossible. No one would say aloud that the real business of government was the redistribution of money from the under-represented to the over-represented, to those with the best lawyers. Elle was a rube when it came to "how things really work." In Estancia she dealt with a different reality. Here things mostly didn't work at all. The well flowed or it didn't. The roof held up under the monsoons or it leaked. Clouds glided past her kitchen window like great ships bound for the New World. What was she but a settler in this timeless desert?

Back to the kitchen for water. Log on the fire. Music?

She put Bach's *Goldberg Variations* on the turntable. Bach taught Latin, wrote a cantata a week for four years, raised a dozen children, played the organ four or five days a week—and wrote the Goldberg Variations. Records—*vinyl*, as he'd called them—had been Elliot's greatest passion— though the music hadn't mattered so much as the purity of its delivery. Elliot had spent thousands of dollars on *state-of-the-art* equipment—turntables and tube amplifiers and pre-amps and an elaborate box covered with sliding switches for something Elliot had called "sonic integration." Elle was an attentive listener. Alone, without a television, she had thousands of records to keep her company— Elliot's records, none with so much as a scratch. Her husband had cultivated a care of his person, house, tools, and inner life that a surgeon might be expected to favor. No room for improvisation in his line of work, though Elle suspected her husband's *fussiness* (as she thought of it) wasn't the effect of his vocation but its cause. What better line of work for a man who laid out his silverware like scalpels, whose suits were a measured three inches apart in the closet, whose view of the world was scrubbed clean of illusions and myths—for much of his life a man of reason, an eighteenth-century humanist, not unlike one-half of her Leopardi, the half that could write four thousand pages of brilliant reflections in a little over two years, who lived in well-concealed despair, deep within a cocoon of melancholy that no one appeared to notice. "Well adapted." That was Elliot. Sure of himself, calm and centered. Boring. Yes, that too. Perhaps Leopardi had been boring as well, though Elle doubted it; the evidence of his poetry suggested otherwise. But what was poetry but a deflection of feeling, a mask one wore to conceal deeper truths? *Concealment.* There was something she needed to remember. Here: the *gigue.* Elliot's favorite moment—a dance too ponderous for any dancer. A song too difficult to sing, words too personal to translate. The trick of language was just enough translucence to cast a shadow. Too much clarity was no good—humankind bearing reality, Footfalls echo in the memory/ Down the passage which we did not take/Towards the door we never opened. *"For years I have been alone here/in darkness."* Alone in darkness.

The record ended and Elle turned it over. Not Gould but Angela Hewitt, a lighter touch, sonorous, understated. Elle's ear wasn't what it once had been. Back at her desk Elle wrote out three versions of the line, none of them pleasing. Then worked on the next stanza, lost in the Italian. The year she'd nearly died Elliot had brought her books, Leopardi, but also Milosz and Neruda, Paz and Baudelaire. "*Giacqui: insensato, attonito,/ Non dimandai conforto/Quasi perduto e morto,/Il cor s'abbandono.*" Elle had complained bitterly—she was a terrible patient. "Lying insensate, not wishing relief, my heart having surrendered…" Had she given up? Cancer, but of one of the minor ones, the kind that in those days was cut out of you—taken away in a stainless steel dish, examined, biopsied, swabs of tissue scrutinized under a microscope, probably all of it burned up in the hospital's bowels, a thin trail of smoke that had once been a length of intestine. Well, God or whoever had provided more than enough. Like horseshoe crabs leaving a galaxy's worth of eggs, nearly all of which were snatched up by shorebirds. Waste was the key to nature. Ill for months, she'd waited a long time with the pain but was "lucky." She'd have preferred something less dramatic: a minor heart attack, something controlled with drugs or a lifestyle change—no more bacon and eggs on Sunday mornings, granola and goat's milk instead of six weeks of recovery and a liquid diet. Extruda? Lactide? A canned concoction that tasted vaguely of coconuts and pineapples, a tropical cocktail packed with vitamins and minerals, endured until the sutures closed, until the ropes of her gut rejoined. Elle hadn't realized how much she'd enjoyed chewing—tearing off a piece of lettuce or the satisfying snap of a carrot. She'd been absurdly young—forty-two. "Where's the luck in that," she'd asked Elliot. "No one gets intestinal cancer." It was a relief to have a doctor handy whom she could berate during the weeks leading up to the surgery. "What sort of arrangement is this, twenty feet of intestine—who needs it? A bit overdone, don't you think?" Elle often complained about the wastefulness of the world. Too many people, stores overstuffed with things no one would ever buy, twenty feet of intestine. "Twenty-eight feet actually." Elliot had come to sit with her when he wasn't working, a thin man dressed in green scrubs, with blue paper booties covering his gardening shoes. In the old days Elle imagined that her husband would have been covered in blood, fresh from sawing off gangrenous legs—was it true men were given shots of brandy and sticks to bite? Elle had wanted to be anesthetized into a black hole. When she woke after three hours she'd felt reborn into a different world, her body was numb, her eyes clouded, her brain scrubbed clean. Who was she? What had happened? This illusion of a stable self turned out to be thin, undone by opioids of some description—Elliot wouldn't tell her anything, afraid that knowledge of possible complications would undo her recovery. For days she drifted back and forth in twilight. This is what death will be she had thought, but going the other way. No memory whatever of the day before or the day of the operation. "That's normal, a trauma to the body disappears into the somatic region of the brain—a deep memory, but not one you have to worry about." Elliot was in his element. He knew what to say, how to be detached—what was the body but a set of problems rectified by medicine? Young Elliot had believed in medicine in the way Jimmy Stewart had believed in politics. Medicine was a toolkit, centuries of empirical knowledge, a respected craft. Bedside manners weren't import-ant. Like most doctors Elle had met—she'd met a few—Elliot was brusque about illness in the way a car mechanic was disinterested in small talk when he changed her oil or rotated her tires. This was partly about concentration, but mostly, Elle knew, central to the brotherhood, the hard-won secrets of doctoring were not to be shared with outsiders. And Elliot was a secretive man to begin with, not sneaky, but self-possessed, self-reliant in the Emersonian sense of making do with the way things were. Unlike her poets, her husband never *yearned*, never sought out ambiguity. Which, Elle knew, had refreshed her. Could she have married a man like Sabo or Leopardi, a man for whom every moment was rich with deeper meanings? No. It would have been unbearable. To the bookshelf. Nemerov. *"There came a moment when you couldn't tell./ And then they clearly flew instead of fell."* That summed the problem up nicely: Elliot was prose and she was poetry, more a mixture than a solution, indissoluble in one another. After her surgery, when Elle had awakened and was beginning to understand the nature of pain, Elliot sat quietly on the edge of her bed, wondering what to do. She couldn't read and had no desire to talk. They sat for hours in silence. Elle thought it might have been the best time of their life together. Oil and water.

Scribbling, reading, talking to herself. "How

would he have read these lines?" *"This inhuman place full of suffering…"* His voice high-pitched and plaintive. His body stooped and bent. A broken tree. An enormous head angled over thin shoulders. Not a hunchback but *deformed*. Kierkegaard too had been misshapen, also alone, eccentric. Had given up Regina, his beloved. Elle couldn't remember why. For God? You couldn't have both. Belief requires self-abrogation, submission. Elle hated biographies. Couldn't bear to read a word about Byron's great aunt or the courses he had failed at St. Paul's. The presumption of writing a life, picking out a few hundred episodes from the millions that made a person. Beauty not of the body—"the worst of all afflictions/old age, in which desire is unfulfilled." And his desire had never been fulfilled. But whose desire is ever fulfilled? Wasn't the notion of "fulfillment" a myth? Who had he loved, and who had loved him? Elliot's reading voice had been deep and rich, but to Elle's ear it lacked inflection. He'd read Homer to her when she came home from the hospital—the *Iliad*, a poem Elle couldn't abide. But it had been restful, sitting on the porch in the warm afternoon sun, slightly abuzz on codeine, listening to stories of Bronze Age massacres. Brain-pans split. Her own voice was a miserable instrument for poetry—too raspy, a smoker's voice, though she'd never smoked. Elle had once read some of her translations in Berkeley on the same stage as Milosz, greatest poet of the century. She knew what the lines sounded like, but what good did that do her? What relationship did the voice have to the mind? Poets sing. "*Ameni inganni.*" She wrote "happy illusions," but crossed it out. "Not at all," Elle said to the window—it was snowing lightly. The sky would change again in a few minutes. She could see the clear glow at the edge of the gray clouds. "Clear delusions." No. He's describing youthful illusions, not delusions, not the same thing. But what was the difference? Lit up, not darkened. Elle got up and walked into the living room where she could see the sky. As a young woman she'd believed in the goodness of her parents, in the endlessness of their lives and of her own, in the benign nature of most other human beings, in the beauty of stories, in the unspoiled grace of the world surrounding her home and school—there were woods and lakes and the ocean wasn't far off and the seasons changed with the kind of predictable consequences that everyone had come to expect. No one Elle knew was rich or poor, and if there were poor people, someone was taking care of them. What were these—delusions? Or illusions? Or truths that changed with time? Maybe there was only one thing, as Leopardi sometimes seemed to think, one thing that can be looked at in different ways, or described variously. Maybe, Elle thought, I'll come around to my illusions again. If youthful, they must certainly be incorrect. Leopardi writing at the ripe old age of twenty-three deplored the delusions of his youth. But time was compressed for him—he must have known he hadn't long to live. What he would think and feel had to be pushed into a tiny space. No one, Elle thought, had lived so intensely. "Beautiful illusions." Elle had seen her own fall away, beginning with her parents' divorce, the bitterness that her mother allowed to consume her spirit—"hardly that!" Elle smirked at the idea of her mother's "spirit." Though a churchgoer, her mother harbored no delusions—divorce had taught her realism. *Realism*: the last refuge of scoundrels. What did Leopardi have to say about realism? Nothing. But he'd written in his notebooks that the more receptive one's organs are to the world, the more attuned to living one is, the greater one's self-love tends to be. Her mother's self-love had nothing to do with sensitivity but with her realism—her not wearing "rose-colored glasses." "Tinted," Elle had said over and over, "you mean to say 'rose-tinted glasses,'" provoking her mother's fury, a woman who scorned correction. "We all wear those glasses," Elle would declare, and her mother walked away to brood, to ask herself why her child was so ungrateful. Elle *was* ungrateful: it was her defining quality. To her parents and husband and son—to her friends, when she had any, to her country, to herself.

It was Casals after all. Her eyes were going. RCA Victor Red Seal. Gratitude was a form of grace, *gratis*, "I rend myself of gratitude and kindness/and become one who despises men," but had he meant it? His "arid life," dried up at twenty-three, alone with his books as Montaigne had been alone with his, but with a great difference: the Frenchman had already lived a full life, married, produced an heir, served his father's memory, his country. His solitude was complacent. Leopardi, having done none of those things, lived alone in agitation and restlessness. Arid life.

At twenty-three, the age at which Leopardi was filling his notebooks, Elle was about to graduate from Smith with a degree in Italian literature. She'd packed her things in a canvas rucksack and flown to Rome for a year. In the top drawer of her desk she had a thick bundle of postcards that she'd mailed home; her mother had saved them for forty years and passed them back to her daughter as she "cleared the decks." Had she said that? A naval metaphor seemed unlikely. A collector of various objects who constantly grew tired of her particular possessions as they ceased to reflect how she was seeing herself in that moment. In her final house, the faux-Spanish mansion tucked away in a small gated community near Ocala—no place really, hot and muggy year round, a golfing town that boasted clean lakes and world-class fishing—Elle's mother had filled her closets with her "hobbies"—Santas and Waterford crystal, editions of Dickens, books stockpiled not for their stories (she never read books) but for the illustrations, photographs of perfect strangers, caricatures, etchings from bygone eras about which Cristina had no curiosity. "That's a copy of Daumier's 'First Class Carriage,'" Elle would say, but this fact possessed no charm for her mother. Who Daumier was, his place in the history of art, his satirical eye—Elle could interest her mother in none of these topics. It was simply an illustration that she had found at the Sunday morning flea market and that had seemed like a bargain. "I love the frame," she would say, and Elle would shrug. Then, with the closets full and the days playing out toward emptiness—her second husband buried—Elle's mother unloaded everything at garage sales and swap meets, mailed boxes of "collectibles" to Elle and Elliot—who in turn unloaded them at Estancia's Goodwill Store, delighting in the knowledge that one of their poor neighbors might walk off with a Waterford carafe for ten bucks. Living in 1500 square feet didn't leave enough room for their own possessions, let alone Cristina's. "You'll remember your trip with the postcards to remind you," her mother had written with her usual disregard for syntax. But it wasn't true. The images of Roman ruins in Sicily, of the Ponte Vecchio, of the Milanese Alps, the slips of yellowed and blurred cardboard had progressively obscured rather than clarified Elle's memories of that year. There'd been a fling in Rome, hours of walking through the Museo Nazionale Romano, peering into churches, reading Sveno and Croce in her bedsit, a train to Prague—the year had become someone else's memory. Here was a photo of her standing in front of Santa Maria degli Angeli—

who, Elle wondered, had taken the photo? Santa Maria had been Michelangelo's last project, the façade a kind of *tromp l'oeil*--no sense at all of the scope of the church from the front, built as it was into the *frigidarium* of the Baths of Diocletian. This, the only picture of Elle from her year in Rome, had been in storage until Elliot's death. She'd found it in the locker they'd rented when their possessions outgrew the tiny house on Granite Hill. In the photograph she saw a slender girl with long chestnut hair wearing a coat—Elle remembered the coat more vividly than the church—a coat her mother had purchased at Saks, a lovely charcoal-gray cashmere that was stolen on the train to Prague, or perhaps from her room in the Hotel Stanislaus in Paris, or someplace else in Europe where, Elle was certain, something else of value had been taken from her as well. Her virginity had been lost earlier, and since she was already hopelessly behind in her translation, nearly ready to renounce the day—it was nearly ten—Elle allowed herself to remember her seduction by Dr. Gabriel Hoffmann, Chairman of the Department of Germanic Studies, not at Smith—Elle knew enough not to foul her nest—but at one of the other Five Colleges. Dr. Hoffman with his alpine face—craggy with acne scars and disfigured by a nose whose pores were studded with blackheads—yet despite his Saturnine looks a man of continental charm and sophistication. Elle had to admit that Hoffmann had been a father-figure, a replica of her absent parent, who was himself a man with bad skin and good manners, an unapproachable melancholic, missing in action from the time Elle was in high school, her late lamented father re-embodied in the gutturals and slightly acidic odor of Gabe Hoffmann, a Goethe scholar of some renown, garrulous and priapistic, an experienced seducer of naïve and virginal Smith girls as well as of his colleagues' wives. Who could say what had led Elle to Dr. Hoffmann's bed? She could, of course. It simply isn't true that one's heart is opaque, that one's wishes and desires remain hidden. She'd wanted experience of the sort that only an older man could provide. Elle had no illusions about this affair now, half-a-century later. It had been awkward and unsatisfying. Sex. They hadn't "made love"—that hideous euphemism. Something else had been made—a mess that took some time to clean up, a sadness that took a long time to heal. It was odd, Elle thought, that she was unromantic as a young woman, and was an unsentimental old woman, a woman whose life had been spent thinking about other people's emotions, poets with their untidy inner lives—all of the feelings she should have felt never took hold of her. Hoffmann had been a bad lover, not in a performative sense—Elle smiled when this word came to her—but once he'd *had* her—again the word seemed so off to her, the notion of being *had*, but what else was it, surely not possession and never any deeper bond, once the act was done her ruddy German professor was transformed into a dull-witted (and hairy) bourgeois worried about where the two of them would have dinner. At least this was how Elle remembered an affair that condemned her to Italian for life—she gave up her German minor for French and never liked the language, though she spoke and read it reasonably well. In a rush the whole sordid business came back to her and then, just as quickly, disappeared. Like opening and shutting a door. Back Elle came to the cold January morning, to the broad and bright room. She would never think of Gabriel Hoffmann again.

Should she walk to clear away the debris? It was too early to go outside. Too cold. But nothing was going as it should. She was a little unhinged this morning, a bit daff. A nice word. To be daffing.

She doffed her coat—a bulky goose down big as a comforter that had belonged to Todd—and went out. The path downhill was icy but worn to the gravel. Elle thought this fact was poetic, making the smooth way rough, but wasn't in the mood to write the line down, if there was a line. Had Leopardi ever seen snow? In Milan, if he'd been there. What she wanted at once was to go back inside, but she pushed on toward No Creek. She was surprised to feel a rasp in her chest—another infection coming on, or the residue of the last—the dry air and wood fires encouraged viruses to settle in her lungs, her great weakness since a case of childhood pneumonia. Her mother, as Elle recalled, had insisted on sending her to school with a cold that led to an infection and a hospital stay. Was that true? Elle thought for the thousandth time that she was wrong never to give her mother the benefit of the doubt. Would Todd forgive her, Elle wondered? The wind came up suddenly and cut into her face and ungloved hands. Surprising how cold it got this far south. But she was a mile above sea level. The high desert, proximity to mountains, slight ripples in the air above the Rockies to the North. By ravens' wings. Todd had forgiven her for her minor lapses, but not, she suspected, for the egregious acts, the ones for which she could not forgive herself. And Elliot, toward whose grave she appeared to be walking—had he forgotten what she had done, or meant it when he said, repeatedly, that he forgave her? What does it mean, Elle wondered, to forgive? Forgive and forget. One never forgets. In any case, she never did. The wounds inflicted in the name of love…who could forget them?

It wouldn't do, Elle thought, to leave this place. She had considered moving to Albuquerque or Denver, but neither appealed to her. A real city would be unaffordable. San Francisco might have been her first choice if she had money, which she didn't, and now it was impossible, she could hardly dig Elliot up and trundle him off to the Pacific. A beautiful city, filled with hustlers. Elliot's headstone was alabaster—hand-carved by Joaquin Soto, an artist whose studio Elle could just make out in the distance. Head of stone. Soto was a beautiful man. Hands like rocks, a long black braid tied with a leather band, wiry and brown, his movements and speech slow. Bad teeth. *Mysterium solvitur animam viventem*. Elliot had insisted upon Latin—why not English or, if a foreign tongue was required, Spanish, a language Elliot spoke fluently, whereas his only Latin was medical. "It sounds right in Latin," he had said. Looking at the inscription now, Elle wondered if living solved life's problems, or if it multiplied them. Said in English, this bromide was patently untrue. Latin's magisterium added luster and a germ of truth to what was ambiguous at best. Elliot hadn't been able to answer the questions posed by living. He'd not had days or weeks on a deathbed to share his thoughts with Elle, nor had he been a man to write personal things down—unlike his wife he'd kept no diaries or journals—his reticence was his most consistent characteristic. He'd died of a stroke, eating dinner, right in front of Elle. They'd been having soup and homemade bread, sitting at the oak table in the kitchen, when Elliot pitched forward, landing face-down in his bowl of beans—alive and laughing one moment, stone-cold dead the next. Elle hadn't anticipated the sudden void in her life. He was only seventy-one when he died. He had retired only a few years before. Bean soup—of all the things she might have made on that night. Elle hated bean soup. Elliot was a fastidious man, proud of his wavy hair and closely trimmed beard. He'd worn lightly starched shirts around the house, Pendleton sweaters, pressed khakis. He'd splashed cologne on this hairy face every morning—he liked the smell of Old Spice—and took care that his eyebrows and nose hairs didn't "get out of hand." He had what Elle thought of as a surgeon's squeamishness about the body's vagaries, its tendency to turn to flab and slouch. "No sense decaying before one must!" Not a slogan likely to catch on in the era of Botox and firm tushes, white teeth and flat stomachs. They had briefly been friends with a cosmetic surgeon and his wife—Kasselbach, Mort and spouse. Each of them taut-faced, their skin parchment thin, but otherwise unremarkable persons. Abigail Kasselbach. Elle had called her AKA since a person so altered seems an alias. Rump like a shelf, horsey. Elle rubbed her arm where she'd been nipped (bitten!) by a cantankerous Indian pony at Monument Valley all those years ago. Abby and Mort. Had Elliot really pitched forward into a bowl of soup or was Elle imagining it? *"The way to understand how to live is to live."* Even in Latin it was a stupid. Banal and untrue. The headstones in the cemetery at Old North Church sported Scripture—Isaiah had been all the vogue in the eighteenth century—"All of our good deeds are as filthy rags." There was a sentiment to take along on one's journey to Zion. The way to understand how to live is to consider dying. To consider the how and when and the why of it. Once that was done you began to live in earnest. Close to the bone. Meaning? Nearer the truth? The uncomfortable truth—Elliot knew more about the physical side of mortality than she, but he never would have thought the truth uncomfortable. Elliot's legacy was the house and the garden, a tangle of blackened sunflowers and rotted tomato plants, grape vines untidily draped over strung wire—they'd come back in the spring with a vitality that never failed to surprise Elle. How could something appear so dead and yet green up in a matter of days? Produce fruit year after year—they left the tiny white-green grapes for the birds that careened around the garden in wild joy (she imagined) and gluttony. She wouldn't plant anything this season— too much work. She'd throw a few sunflower seeds in the ground as a tribute to Elliot. A house and a garden, some canned vegetables still stacked in the root cellar. She'd never eat them—she hated home canning, was terrified of botulism, opening a jar of rotted corn or peas. A house, an untidy house that looked about to fall down, at least it did from here, seen from the flat stretch among the elms and cottonwoods where Elliot was interred. A freezing wind lifted Elle's hair, white and thin, lifted it and refused to put it down again. She pulled it back and tied it to her head. She wasn't cold any longer. What else besides the house and some memories? Real estate and forty-six years. A son. Another son buried in Newton. The one they hadn't planned on and then wouldn't discuss. Her fault. Does the word "careless" apply in such cases? *Di tua natura arcana.* Dearest love, little boy. Born too soon, like the sparrow fledglings that turn up in the grass, pink with spindly gray feathers, hopping about, enormous unopened eyes, hopeless. How little was left when a life was over. The memories would die with her and before long someone else would be living in the house—Todd hated Estancia and would sell the "pile" and invest the profits in a hedge fund and make a killing. No doubt about it, her son was a whiz when it came to money—"a magician" Elliot had called Todd, though he wouldn't trust his son with any of his and Elle's savings. He'd preferred to earn 2% at the Wells Fargo in Moriarty to assuming the risks that Todd took with his own considerable portfolio. Elliot hadn't cared about money; their son thought of little else. And if Todd had children they'd proba-bly live on a commune. That's the way of world—Elle said it aloud, "*the way of the world.*" A phrase that seemed so wise and said so little. In twenty years, maybe ten, someone would discover Elliot's canned corn in the cellar, the bins of dried rosemary and basil. The meaning of a life is the living of a life. There's no mystery at all. It's a poet's conceit that there is anything to it other than this— walking on a cold morning. Mailing a letter in town during a snowstorm. Sipping a cup of tea as rain battered the tin roof. Maybe Elliot was onto something. Was it Horace or Pliny? Elle hadn't done well in Latin—too churchy. She would have a line from Leopardi—who else? She was inclined toward cremation and scattering—up on the top of the Sandias would be lovely—rather than a spot near Elliot—let him rest without her. Then again the idea of fire was agonizing. What if the dead felt the flames—did they use flames, or was the process flameless, microwaves amped up to the point where the body combusted to ash, instantaneous and effi- cient, like bread incinerated in the toaster? She'd be ash in any case. The whole thing would be ash. Then, what? Hydrogen and helium. Never noth- ing. Of that one could be certain. *It* would go on forever, a horrifying thought. Flames far better than worms. Maggots. She'd seen pictures of the dead, of the Japanese on some island where they'd fought to the death. Iwo Jima or Okinawa. Her father had a book of *Life* magazine war photos. He'd given it to her. There had been some instructions about "facing the facts" or perhaps he had told her that she needed to understand the brutality of war. He'd been a part-time pacifist, a Unitarian who'd admired King and Gandhi, a Republican who cheated on his taxes and voted for Ike and Nixon. He'd admired the Japanese, their resilience, and their sense of honor. Hairy Carrie. Honor seemed not to go with pacifism, which, Elle supposed, was her father's chief problem believing in what he professed to believe in. Commie Kazis. It had all been a muddle to Elle, the little dinnertime speeches on The War. Morality, according to Father, was to assent with the will. She remembered that from Aquinas: the assent of one's will to sin. In Augustine the sin was a given; in Aquinas it was willed. Believing meant saying yes to something without thinking too much about what would be entailed. Leopardi assented to an idea "like a tower in an empty field." For her father assent was scattered about like spring snow. Gandhi and Nixon had seemed a stretch to Elle even when she was a young woman and eager to give her father the benefit of the doubt. He had admired their spunk—"Nixon ended the war!" Maggots feasting on flesh. The smell of decay. Elliot had taken her to see an autopsy—she'd gagged up her oatmeal. They said that in mystery novels—"He recognized the unmistakable smell of a dead body," a corpse. *Corpus est corpus meum*, or something like that. A corpse in the copse. In the Scandinavian mysteries that Elliot had preferred the corpse was always preserved in snow—terrible to imagine—the face gray-blue, the limbs at attention, frozen, "the knife handle was plain wood, sticking from his back like a," like a what? No metaphor for something like a knife in the back. Metaphors only came in handy when there was ambiguity. Was Elliot frozen under the trees? Elle couldn't push the thought of him out of her mind—he was wearing a suit. Blue she thought, or maybe gray. And a red tie—of that she was certain. Todd had handled the dressing, Todd and the son of the undertaker. The taker under. Then: *Hoc est corpus meum*. Bread instead of flesh seemed sensible—a wafer.

Elle felt dizzy again. Did she have a tumor? Low blood sugar? No telling, and there was no way she'd go to the doctor. Maybe it was the cold. The wind nearly lifted her off her feet. She'd had more than one bite of Jesus. He had stuck to the roof of her mouth and she'd been tempted to peel it off with her finger. But you couldn't touch it. It was God, so you'd die. She'd been a child, no more than seven or eight, and her mother had told her the meaning of the Eucharist—she'd thought of those Bela Lugosi movies she'd seen on WPIX, the ones where the mad doctor had ingested a steamy potion designed to enhance his powers—what powers?— she couldn't recall—but instead he grasps his throat and turns into a hideous demon. So she'd waited for the wafer to dissolve, summoned up saliva by the pint to wash it down—and then what? Did it make its way through the very intestine that Dr. Carlton, Elliot's gastroenterologist colleague, would cut out of her thirty-odd years later? Did she expel it, flush it away, or did it—as her mother claimed—become a part of her soul, nourishment for the invisible Elle, the real Elle, the one who would have eternal life if she would go to church and learn her catechism. In truth, neither her Catholic mother or Unitarian/ agnostic/Republican father had much interest in the afterlife—her mother hated getting up early on Sunday, "dressing," and would only go on Christmas and Easter, a major production requiring a new outfit, a hat, gloves, taking Elle with her so that she could leave Mass early, claiming—truthfully—that the child was too restless for her to remain until the end. Her father read the *Times* on Sunday mornings with his bacon and eggs. He called the two runny sunny-side up eggs his "sacramental meal," mocking his wife's Sunday guilt. Elle had preferred playing with her paper dolls. Cutting them out and folding the tabbed outfits onto their bodies, over their undergarments, long white bloomers and modest tee shirts. No eternal life, and, please—Elle thought now—no maggots. But a marker—"*Che vuol dir questa/Solitudine immensa?*" Not that. The meaning of this great emptiness is no meaning at all. Elle was certain of this—no meaning at all. The very idea that the world had meaning seemed idiotic—who could think such a thing? What could anyone attach to the vast empty sky—she could see sixty miles to the east and north and south—the Manzano mountains blocked her western view— other than the momentary pleasure of standing beneath it?

Getting colder. Why this constant clawing after meaning—and what would meaning even look like once you found it? Another sentence? A poem? A brilliant equation like E=mc^2—The Well-Tempered Klavier? The meaning of life might be Newton's F=ma, the only physics she remembered from high school. Or a great resounding A (her favorite key), tuning the orchestra of the universe. Why not just settle for what there was to see: *io che sono*? Her favorite of his poems, bucolic. That was the word she wanted. Bucolic. Elle turned from Elliot's grave without saying goodbye. It was a superstition of hers, not turning away but saying something—"I'll be back," or, absurdly, "Be well." In her haste she forgot to say anything at all. She passed back up the hill to the house shivering, with other things on her mind. Later in the day she would regret turning her back on Elliot, and it would feel like another in a lifetime of betrayals.

Working at last. The house was warm but Elle wore her gloves out of habit. Fingers cut away, clutching her pen, a graduation gift from her mother. *Canti* to her left; long sheets of yellow paper on her right; dictionaries open all around; Telemann on the stereo. The best moment of the day, settling to work, when there was hope that things would go well, when progress would be made, before the inevitable disappointments of the afternoon. Above her desk a portrait, Leopardi as a young man—attractive, Elle thought, with an open face and compassionate eyes. We see what we want in other people, no doubt about that, but Elle was sure she would have enjoyed walking along the Potenza with him, discussing philology, about which Elle knew little, though she was an attentive listener.

Piansi spogliata, esanime
Fatta per me la vita;
La terra inaridita,
Chiusa in eterno gel…

Elle wrote her first draft in prose: "I cried because life to me was empty; the earth arid/dried up, shut in eternal ice." Elle thought that ice was the perfect Italian metaphor for sorrow—Satan sunk to his midsection in a sea of ice—warm Adriatic breezes that must have blown through the open windows at Recanati. What had brought Leopardi to the verge of despair, and how did he recover? Elle thought she understood the loneliness of the poet, the harsh theology of his father, the burden of his diseased body, his obsession with learning. But there was something more lying behind *Il Risorgimento*, something deeper than biography. But wasn't there always something deeper?

I wept for the emptiness of my life,
The arid earth, locked in eternal ice.

Of course "ice" and "arid" were a problem—but then the Arctic was a desert, so perhaps not. The dry plain of ice. Tundra and swirling wind. Outside in the now fully risen sun (low arched, bending toward the southern plains) water ran from snowmelt—down the *canales*, splattering against the house. Elle listened and imagined the voice of the poet in the tumble of melted ice.

I cried for my empty life,
barren and dead,
for the arid earth
frozen in unmelting ice.

Worse still. Elle flipped through the *Canti* to another poem. She translated as she read: "There were times I left my beloved books and the pages I had labored over during the best years of my young life...I listened from my father's balcony to

the sound of your voice…" The lure of words—
Elle felt it deeply. When she had been in college
there was nothing for her but her studies; and after,
before and during her marriage, poetry had pulled
her away from other people—from her mother and
then from her husband and child. She'd been looking for something during those years, but what was
it? Now that she was alone and able to do as she
wished it was less clear to her why she had hidden
herself in the voices of poets: Baudelaire, Rimbaud,
Novalis, Heine, Trackl—dead of a drug overdose
before he was thirty—all of these poets melancholy figures, young men given to self destruction.
And Elle, an upright Anglo-Saxon girl from no
where—Smith grad, non-smoker, virtual teeto-
taler, non-inhaler of pot—it unhinged her to lose
control—wife and mother and widow and hermit,
why should she have devoted so much of her life to
these shadowy figures, Leopardi the most compel-
ling of them, the most illusive and unknowable of
all? It was nonsense. A young man's sadness. He'd
had a tyrannical father and an intense sensibility—
what did this have to do with Elle, a woman with
her own problems?

I wept for the emptiness of my life.

and for an arid earth locked in ice.

Turning words over sometimes seemed as useless as digging a hole and filling it in. Elliot had made a difference; he'd cured people, saved lives, lost a few along the way, but what is medicine if not triage? "You can't win them all" Elliot would cheerfully sing (to the tune of "Stormy Weather") over his Martini, though he didn't mean it, and couldn't bear the thought of failure. At Sibley and GW he had been the most highly sought after thoracic surgeon—Senators and Congressmen and Cabinet members had summoned him away from his NIH office when they needed cutting. Elle had found her husband's attachment to the chest cavities of the powerful distasteful, though she couldn't have said why. The money had come in handy. Todd had gone to Yale and Harvard Business School; they'd lived in a lovely home in a good neighborhood and never wanted for anything. Which was why Elle had been eager to get out, to move to Utah or Wyoming or New Mexico, someplace far from the life she had lived in the East, someplace where they could regroup—"find ourselves"—a phrase that fit Elle but not Elliot, though he had his own reasons for wanting to get away. Elle had been cruel to Elliot at the time of their move, insistent on getting her own way. She *would* leave Washington, and she remembered a dreary Sunday afternoon argument during which she had threatened to move to New Mexico by herself. Elliot had friends and belonged to a country club. He golfed on Saturdays with his fellow doctors. He had a girlfriend—of this Elle was certain—a woman he kept in a condo in Silver Spring and visited twice a week. "*Quando sovviemmi di cotanta speme,/Un affetto mi preme/ Acerbo e sconsolato.*"

I cried out at life's emptiness
and the barren earth, locked in ice.

The lessons of her mother's life should have been sufficient to divest her of illusions. She could feel it even now, years after the fact, Elliot's leaving her alone at night, his distraction when they spoke, the sudden care he took in his unassuming appearance. These things happen. "I wept for life's bitterness, for the earth, dried out and yet frozen in ice." Who but the diseased Italian atheist could have understood how she felt? Sitting alone in a silence unlike any she had known in her Eastern life—always in Boston or Washington the braying of traffic, human voices drifting in from the street, jets rising or descending—here there nothing but the final notes of Jean-Pierre Rampal's flute. A silence not unlike that of the house at Wellfleet—summer evenings, no dog to run in the oat grass, the silence Hopper had painted. Elle closed her eyes and conjured the ramshackle graying clapboard of the house on the dunes—her favorite house. Leopardi had been born into a family home, fifteen miles from the Adriatic, the smell of the sea—born in a house his family had lived in from time immemorial, his father a grandee, minor royalty in a country where nobility mattered, his library monumental—architectural continuity and majesty being the single advantage of aristocracy. Leopardi's father Monaldo had joined a great pilgrimage to the home of the Virgin at Loreto the year Bonaparte had ridden into Rome to carry off Italy's treasures. Plunder and republicanism had coexisted even then. The horses on the dusty track, wagons with solid oaken wheels, the clatter of swords on leather, sweat and bodyheat, the sky bleached white. On Cape Cod, Elle had risen before dawn to sip her coffee on the porch overlooking the dunes—the sun rose from the ocean with mythic power, and Elle wouldn't have been shocked to see the Achaean fleet in full sail, bound for the coast of Asia Minor. Not wine-dark but white-capped, though the Aegean had been calm as a lake the summer she had travelled from Piraeus to Crete—a long night spent passing a bottle of Retsina from hand to hand, at dawn the long low coast from which kings had embarked for millennia to trade and make war and for the sheer wonder of being alive in Middle Earth. While Elliot slept she would walk along the edge of the beach, the water ice-cold in August, the dunlins and turnstones picking at the edge of the waves. It was in Wellfleet, in a house that she had stocked with Aldo Leopold and Thoreau and May Sarton that Elle learned solitude. Elliot would stay for weekends but work called him back to Boston, so Elle was able to pass her summers alone with Todd or, once he'd been shipped off to summer camp, entirely alone. It was in the Wellfleet house that she had done her work on Sabra and written some of her best verses. Her poems were of that place and time, and hadn't lasted. The best writers weren't attached to places but to language. Leop-ardi excepted. He was tied to nothing. He rose above Italy and Recanati, above language, above his personal history—he belonged, Elle thought, to nothing.

⸺⁓⸺

"How melodramatic." She was running on too quickly. Her eyes felt unfocused, her hand trembling ever so slightly. Elle allowed herself five minutes (timed on the big brown school clock over her desk) to brood about the deeper meanings of her life's geography, her travels. Her author had believed that history rendered human affairs uniform, washing away what turned out to be unimportant differences. No Hegelian Self for Leopardi, no Spirit brooding over the otherwise incomprehensible deeds of Man. No, he was a natural aristocrat of the human spirit, the last humanist. The last human.

Back to Wellfleet. She had loved to feel the crust of salt on her legs as she walked the beach at sunrise. The wind seldom ceased its howl. The bars in Provincetown, full of gay men who had made her feel welcome. She'd drink Old Fashioneds and throw darts with boys from New York. Tipsy, she would ask young men about O'Neill and George Cram Cook—had they heard of "The Emperor Jones"? Some had, remarkable now that she thought of it, and she felt warm remembering long nights of good talk with total strangers. At her house the weathervane above the chimney had turned in unending circles—gulls flew against the eastern breeze, rising awkwardly on thermals, alighting in the spot from which they arose. The wind! Struggling against a stiff offshore breeze, landing in the spot from which you had ascended, gulls a symbol (Elle remembered now) of the fruitlessness of effort. And: Leopardi understood, as no one after him had—(stalled again!) she was in the mood for absolutes—that to live is to partake of a rich inner world. And the richness of language, a gift of God, was created for us to say something about that world. As for the rest: all of it was nonsense. Science, with its fetish for clarity, for truth, had come along and destroyed the humane impulse. Not poetry but eugenics, not beauty but biology. Elle knew that no feeling can be expressed in a word designed to fit that feeling—language is adaptation. She looked up the passage in the Zibaldone: *the mind in discovering new ideas embodies them in the language of what is known and perceptible*—He'd believed that all words belong to something else and are loaned out to include what hasn't been thought of before. Meaning is the ocean, language the small glass that cannot contain it—or is it the other around? And what about the invisible depths of ambiguity, of feeling that runs cold beneath the surface? What vessel could hold that?

> The Day was a desert,
> The night silent and dark
> The moon had vanished
> With the stars in the sky

It was in the back bedroom of the Wellfleet house that Elle had first slept with a man who was not her husband. It wasn't only solitude that she learned on the summer beaches of Cape Cod. She had wanted to be the first to break the vow of exclusivity—to do so preemptively—that way (she reasoned) she could never be hurt. Or perhaps then she could never blame Elliot for anything— what better way to find happiness with someone than to betray him? Here in the *Zibaldone* was the line she wanted: "At death the naked soul will fly once more to God." Right out of Plato or Thomas Aquinas, the soul a diminutive ghost exiting the nostrils, the family huddled around the bedside, awaiting the reading of the will. Who was that? Mr. Featherstone?

Scenes from Masterpiece Theatre—television

for those who hated television—the candles and bedclothes, the stench of unwashed linens and flesh, wizened, *adustezza*. Thomas Aquinas and his odorless ideas in support of one idea—building a human mind to teach a single sentence—"God exists." She'd met Thomas Whitlow in Boston—he'd lived with his wife and two children not far from Elle's own cozy Back Bay row home. She and Elliot had moved with each election, getting closer to the *Hub* (they'd had pronounced the word with all the wry self-satisfaction of the liberal classes) but really just spending more money. Elle saw Thomas from time to time at the market, at First Church on the rare occasions she would compel Elliot and Todd to dress and attend services, at Symphony Hall where the Whitlow's had held tickets for three generations. Once she and Thomas had shared a mid-program Evian and chatted about the soloist's décolleté. Thomas was in finance. Elliot disliked him on principle. No man, in Elliot's view, should make a living moving money around, especially other people's money. "But we have money in an account ourselves," and it did move around, from bonds to stocks to futures—a grand notion, futures—and the money came over time to be more money, and it was with this fluid capital that Elliot had bought the house in Wellfleet in whose back bedroom Elle had allowed herself to be seduced by a man who was older and less interesting than her husband. Sitting now, so many years later—was Thomas still alive?—Elle thought that if he were he would be no different in substance than the man she had known long ago, the lack of change, rather than change's inevitability, being the essence of a certain class of New Englanders, Brahmins who never worked but curated money that came to them with fine china and the family silver, money that likely originated on a slave-labor plantation in the Caribbean or Virginia, and—such a long and uncharitable thought!—having lived their three-score and ten years, they went on to rest eternally at Old North Church right next to others of their kind. Filthy rags of our lives. In Estancia—the memory now obsessive—Elle was at a loss as to why she had allowed herself to have carnal relations with such a man. She had a notebook someplace from that summer—it was 1980 or one or two—but she didn't need to look for the notebook to remember the details. "Allowed myself." Sounded nice, but it hadn't been like that at all. She was the instigator. Elle reached for a blank sheet of paper and tried a couple of lines: *Dark salt air pushed through the eaves/there an edge of light pierced/noon's unaccustomed darkness*…and he cried on my stomach afterward. He loved his wife. Well, I loved Elliot. Weepy men, Elle thought, were the worst. Thomas had been alone for weeks, recovering from overwork, stress. There'd been some problems with the SEC, his EKG. Always there were problems. Happy people didn't have affairs. His wife and children were in Boston, all of them going to school. She was a professor at Harvard. Law or dentistry. Something practical, Elle remembered. Anyway they had money, oodles of money, a townhouse in Back Bay and a home in Wellfleet. Something in London. He'd showed off pictures of his houses and condos as if they young children who'd won the Latin Prize. Walking on the beach, Elle would sometimes pass Thomas—Tom—and they would stop and chat about the weather or their plans for the summer. The best place to get fresh seafood. Tom was a big man, muscular and fleshy—he described himself as a *gourmand*, a word Elle disliked for its sound and associations—*gurdus*—he wasn't fat, but he did talk far too often and at great length about meals he'd enjoyed. He'd wistfully remember a plate of oysters consumed at Regency

Seafood six months before, and Elle would think how idiotic it was to rhapsodize over a meal. Then again Tom was attentive to her, interested in her work, a "serious reader" of poetry. How had it happened? Elle couldn't remember finding Tom attractive or especially intelligent—he was the sort of man with whom she might enjoy a drink—nothing else. But conditions had been right, or wrong, and she had invited him to look at some books or to listen to records, and things had gotten out of hand. Who had seduced whom? *Seduced*—a lovely word—as in *led apart*. Removed her from duty. How moralistic the Latins were, how wonderfully precise. All these years later Elle couldn't remember anything except the post-coital tears and her own feeling of being far removed from the scene. It had been a sunny day. Cool, nippy, as it sometimes was in mid-summer. Always on the Cape there was the feeling of something ending—the season, the peace one felt on the day of arrival, knowing that all too soon it would be time to empty the drawers that stuck in July and slid open easily a month later. There would be the question of whether or not to wash and pack the shells collected on afternoon walks, what to do with the perishables—should one bother carrying them across the way to the

Girards, the old couple who lived in Wellfleet year round? But that meant conversation, and Elle never felt up to it. So the bread and milk and orange juice went in the garbage and down the sink and the shells were pushed into a cabinet in the laundry room along with last year's shells and the board games (Scrabble, Parcheesi), unused again this summer. Later on, a decade post-Thomas, Mr. Girard died in some unusual and capricious fashion—how? Was it the notorious Cape undertow? Or was it Girard who had stepped on a rusty nail and died of sepsis? Everyone was dying of sepsis these days. If you went to the hospital with a cold you came out dead. The sex couldn't have meant much to either of them, as they hadn't kept going. Was it three times? The first, unplanned, and then two consecutive Sunday eve-nings when the spouses had returned to the city. Was that right? How could one forget such a thing? Then again, why would one remember? She had hated the sneaking about. But not the adrenaline rush one felt thinking about doing it—taking a quick shower, tidying up, chilling a bottle of white wine. Putting the diaphragm in; squatting in the kitchen (it was dusk, still cool), hiking up her dress, an oper-ation she'd never been very good at, unfolding the latex and the sensible dollop of spermicide. A tingle down there, pressure that wasn't unpleasant. That was all it was—friction, pressure dexterously applied over a varying length of time—blood vessels dilating, nerves at attention, hormones awakened—human something gonadotropin. Elliot had told her when they first discovered that she had made some error with her "precautions." That wasn't Todd, but the other one, the one who hadn't quite had it in him to live. Pressure, angles, thrust. It sounded, she thought, like aerodynamics, as if she were a helicopter. How had it felt *exactly*? So many years had passed since she'd had sex with anyone, including herself, that she couldn't recall the details. Women wanted intimacy, wasn't that what was said? Men wanted pleasure. Such nonsense. Pleasure is what we all want and live for, with some slight neurotic variations—monks and nuns and psychopaths. Virginal recluse. Old maid. Elle thought it must have been twice, not three times. Day or night? Sun or rain? Was there anything in life more likely to end in disappointment? When Gertie arose Mr. Leopold Bloom noticed that she was lame and he was repelled. Swift mentioned in a terrible poem (heroic couplets) that sweet what's-her-name shat. Or there was a mole you hadn't noticed before. A smell from down under—someone hadn't wiped or bathed or was prone to perspire in the summer's heat. That was it in a nutshell—a disappointment. Twice: two Sundays in July or August. Between 7 and 8:30 p.m. He would be gone by 9, lingering for an hour after the sex out of politeness. The definition of a gentleman: he doesn't copulate and run (even to herself Elle couldn't bear the harsh fricatives of sex). He would be hungry since Elle hadn't thought to make food. He enjoyed watching the Red Sox on television when his wife wasn't around. He smoked cigars—reeked of them—but wasn't permitted to smoke in front of his children. Elle was making some of this up. He was heavy on her, dead weight. Elliot liked being underneath. If she had been a writer she might have written a sad story about this affair of hers, called it love in the dunes. Duned love. A woman poet with tenure at Harvard would get a sonnet sequence out of the two copulations—probably win the Pulitzer Prize. It had been a tree limb that killed Mr. Girard. That was it. He'd gone walking on a windy day and been struck flush on the head. The next day she had told Tom she couldn't see him again. She said she felt guilty but she hadn't. She hadn't wanted to complicate her life—one husband and one child were enough. A few days after her last meeting with Tom she had phoned Elliot in the city and asked him to come out to the Cape for the night. He was busy, but she made it clear that the matter was urgent so he drove down and had been, Elle recalled, in a foul humor when she told him that she had slept with an acquaintance of theirs. Elliot asked who and Elle told him at once, that she and Thomas Whitlow had been involved but no longer were, or would be, and that he, Elliot had nothing to worry about. Elle cringed at the memory of those words, "You have nothing to worry about." Elliot said that he knew perfectly well that he had a good deal to worry about since his wife had *fucked*—he had said "fucked," a word Elliot had never before been heard to utter—an absurd WASP whose only achievement in life had been inheriting his father's money. And that was all she could remember. End of story. Not an original or especially interesting one. Who hasn't, Elle asked herself now, had a stupid and pointless love affair and been sorry and eventually forgiven? Well, plenty of people. Most people. Was it because, as Elliot had said, she "fancied herself an artist,"—this had hurt—and that artists (he'd said the word with the precise intonation of someone saying "phonies") the sort of people who had extra-marital affairs? Elle had wept, despite her promise to herself that she would not weep and not be contrite, her absurd sense that it was possible to tell your husband you had been intimate with someone else and still maintain the fiction of mutual respect and reasonableness. How the roles were reversed! It wasn't Elliot confessing infidelity to his wife, but Elle—homely, bookish, solitary—who had "crept about with a loutish fool." If Elliot had been someone else he might have struck her—he was that angry—but instead he poured a third drink (cheap Scotch, clear proof that he was *very* upset) and then he "stormed out," as Elle put it to herself now. She remembered vividly that Elliot had slammed the front door hard enough to break the glass. Elle had cut her finger picking up the shards, blood and tears mingling on the sensible threadbare carpet Elliot had tacked down by the front door. Never had Elle felt so terrible, or missed her husband so much, or realized so vividly the importance of giving up her illusions. There had been a trial separation that autumn. Elliot moved to an apartment close to work, leaving Elle the house and car and Todd. Did this in fact occur? It seemed plausible. And if it had happened in this way, the arrangement would have suited Elliot. Given him a much needed lift. He could read the *Times* and talk out loud to the idiots who wrote the editorials. Play his records non-stop and at high volume. Men were made for trial separations. Having it both ways—time with the kid, phone calls to the not-completely-estranged wife. On the other hand Elle imagined that being alone with Todd would have been unbearable. Full-time mothering wasn't the sort of thing Elle was good at—if ever anyone had been designed for part-time mothering, it was Elle. Todd was a handful—he was thirteen that autumn, and angry with his mother for driving his father out of the house. Their lives became a soap opera. Had this happened to her, or to her mother? The separation, the angry child—was it her or Todd? The memory was a muddle. No wonder Leopardi hadn't married; he loathed bathos. Affairs, weepy confessions, estrangement and separation, mother with angry adolescent. All that was needed was a suicide—Thomas, after confessing to his wife, might have shot himself. He was too rich for guns, more likely some arrangement with the tailpipe—suffocation in the garage among his (Elle imagined it) skis and tarp-shrouded Porsche, the power tools that he never used, a riding mower he never rode and fly-fishing equipment still in its boxes. He would have had to consume a great deal of single malt before the deed, but no cashmere coat—dear Anne Sexton wore one, or was it a mink, the perfect suicide dress. He would have done the deed in kakis and a pink button-down shirt, left a scribbled note forgiving Elle and Elliot and his wife the professor. He couldn't, he would write, live with the guilt. But who, Elle wondered at her desk, the sun already growing dim, didn't live with their guilt? But of course Thomas hadn't killed himself. In fact, he was elected to the Boston City Council in 1990. Elle read it in the Washington Post.

Elle went to the living room to stoke the fire. She was shivering. How cold was it? She could put on NPR, but wasn't in the mood for those soothing voices. Why did they have to whisper? There was a thermometer nailed to the outside doorpost, but it had been broken for at least a decade. Elle guessed it was in the teens; a whisper of snow had begun to fall; the porch was covered in granular white, the kind of snow that came when it was deeply cold. Let it snow. Elle had nowhere to go. Over the Christmas holiday just past Todd had invited her to his condo in Miami Beach, but she had declined, pleading the pressing deadline she faced (there was no deadline), a bad cold (ditto), and the desire to remain close to home. It was better to be here, wrapped in two sweaters, watching the faint sunlight angle toward Sierra Blanca, the white top of which was often, though not now, visible from her great window.

Leopardi had died a virgin. He felt things deeply, but was denied the pleasure of physical love. Or maybe there were no pleasures to be denied, or the pleasures are overrated. Perhaps he'd been fortunate. Pleasure was always diluted by pain. Longing and loss were as much a part of love as intimacy, maybe more. Elle went back into the study and searched among the most ancient of her paperbacks for a tattered copy of *Symposium*, a book she'd first read at Smith and reread many times since. Leopardi had read it in Greek and was offended. He found the Greeks suspect for their literary and mythological preoccupation with *pederastia*, that "infamous act" as he called it. His objections felt as much aesthetic as moral—nothing upset Leopardi like the misuse of language. Had he been a virgin? What was all the fuss about? With Thomas, with Elliot, a few others—a bit of pleasure that quickly passed. More regret than joy, as much loneliness as intimacy. Leopardi had Ranieri, as devoted as a wife, dear Ranieri who had stayed with him until the end. Ranieri spent hours staring into the coffin that held the rotted flesh and calcifying bones of Leopardi. Devotion indeed. Elle shuddered at the thought of disinterring Elliot, prying open his coffin, and weeping over at his rag-draped bones. The service had been well attended. Two dozen former colleagues stood in the chapel at Frick's and shared recollections of Elliot's competence, his kindness, and his "fundamental humanity," a phrase that had stuck with Elle for weeks afterward and still puzzled her. What part of our humanity was fundamental? Was it Elliot's competence or his kindness—or something else? Surely not his vivacity or his high spirits as those were long gone by the time he died. No one who had known him in Boston or Bethesda had visited Estancia. He was a different man living in a village than he had been living in a city or a suburb. Stages on life's way. "Fundamental humanity," as in that without which one cannot be thought of as fully human. And what were those qualities? Elle wondered if she were fundamentally human, or only marginally so. One couldn't help but worry about such a thing. She could feel that some kind of reckoning wasn't far off, a tabulation of the pluses and minuses of her life. How would she fare? A morbid thought. Elliot hadn't a minute to tally his life—perhaps he'd done so when she wasn't paying attention. The older you get the more faith you put in snapshots and diaries, in saving letters and postcards—saying to yourself that "you'll come back to them," which you don't, it's just that after a certain point every sign of your having lived needs preserving. Was there an Elliot diary someplace? Elle couldn't remember what she'd done with her husband's papers. In the storage shed, in the attic, or in one of the closets—she would have to go through them all at some point. When he died he'd been saying something about medicine, about an article he'd just read. "The thing is El, surgery will be obsolete in another twenty years" and then something else; she couldn't recall what. He might not even have said this—she may have imagined a conversation that never took place, or substituted an earlier conversation to ease his going—it was as if he'd walked out the door and driven away, never to return. Like her father saying he needed cigarettes, kissing her on the forehead and disappearing for six months. Her mother wouldn't answer any questions. "Where's Dad?" And Cristina would say, "He's taking a trip," which wasn't untrue, but didn't help a nine-year-old understand the silence in the house, the absence. When some people leave the room—her father was one—it's was like there was a hole in the air. She could smell his cologne in the bathroom. There was his toothbrush, his comb, a stray hair caught in the narrow teeth. He'd taken nothing, so desperate was he to leave. Or to return. *Vive quel foco ancor, vive l'affetto*, yes the fire still burns, if dimly, and if not love, then memory. Elle wondered if "fundamental humanity" included undying love. Had Elliot loved her on that final day and evening? Those last years when they were together day and night, sequestered in their small house on the edge of the desert, the two of them like twinned anchorites. She supposed he had, but she would never know. And knowing wouldn't make any difference.

Leopardi, at twenty-one, wasn't distracted by love. He planned to compose religious poems—poems on the centrality of the cross, a ghastly thought. She'd seen lots of them—crosses, not poems—in the north, in the pueblos around the *Sanctuario* of the Blessed Virgin in Chimayo, men carrying full-sized crosses, half-naked, a few crowned with real thorns. Reenactment of a scene no one could imagine, about which nothing reliable was known. Elle couldn't understand how such a story could move an intelligent person, no matter what the circumstances of his upbringing. In one guise Elle supposed that Leopardi was the Paschal Lamb. Given to suffering, offering it to God. His theories in *Zibaldone*, all tending toward an explanation of unhappiness. *If only we were still living in a state of nature*, he wrote. But what did that mean? Where did he *think* we lived? What had Freud written? Man, a prosthetic god? Don all the modern gadgets available and you're still an animal. It was obscene to think that a man's torture and death could expiate all the evils of history. Evil to end evil, suffering to end suffering? What possible sense could such an idea make? It wasn't even moral—agreeing to slice open your son's throat because you'd heard a voice? What did Leopardi do with this problem, with the inadequacy of the sacrifice in the face of the sins? He had his own Christ fantasy—nothing put Elle off more than poets who thought of themselves as martyrs to art or love or mankind. *Pero ch'esser beato/ Negro ai mortali e nega a' morti il fato*—since fate forbids happiness for the living and the dead. Elle opened the Meridiani edition to "Chorus of the Dead," a poem she knew intimately. "Inevitable, empty years." But this was wrong. It wasn't fate that stood in the way of happiness, nor were the years tedious and empty. But that was the beauty of the poem—it betrayed its own subject. In these two-dozen lines was the refutation of Leopardi's pessimism: his genius overcame his fate. Her own life had been a struggle, but she never felt anything had been fated. If anything, she'd felt confounded by choices, by the burden of her self. There were times when Elle believed that the forces arrayed against life were overwhelming. Nonetheless, her "fundamental humanity" had aligned itself against what her poet most hoped for, the solace of faith. How could she be true to herself and to him? What she renounced is what he most loved—"his emotions remained essentially Christian," he yearned for naked truth, rejected consolation, lived close to the bone—to what was fundamental—to language—its limits were the limits of his life.

The phone rang. It did so once or twice a month and was always Todd or Lucy checking to see if the old lady was still alive. Elle let it ring. She didn't mind a chat with Lucy—the girl's English was charming, full of pitching and rolling vowels, like boats churning on a sea of tones. Boat phonemes. Elle had taken a year of Mandarin and never progressed beyond the problems of making the proper sounds. Turning *Mao* into a cat. She had been touched by her daughter-in-law's skill at calligraphy, and felt a rush of delight when she received hand-drawn invitations to Chinese New

Year Parties in New York or Beijing. Needless to say, she never attended. Even when she and Elliot were living in Bethesda, Elle had refused to take the train to Manhattan. Elliot made the trip by himself. "I hate the city" was something Elle was apt to repeat months before there was any invitation—an inoculation against having to pass a weekend in Todd's Upper East Side apartment among his wealthy and entitled friends. Elle's snobbery was annoying to Elliot and to Todd. It was incomprehensible that an educated woman would despise the class of people most likely to buy her books, those who "gave a shit" (Todd's words) about poetry. Maybe she felt inferior? Todd's brownstone was on East 87th Street, around the corner from the Guggenheim, a museum that gave Elle vertigo. "But they're friends of our son. Why won't you do this for him?" This was the wrong question. She had done something for Todd. Once was enough. Todd seldom came to them. "He doesn't visit us." which wasn't true. Todd and Lucy sometimes came at Christmas. The visits weren't always a success. Todd wanted a tree; Todd wanted a wreath and lights; Todd wanted a turkey dinner. Not just a tree, but a fresh-cut spruce; not only turkey, but "all the trimmings." "Since when," Elle had asked, "have you enjoyed a traditional Christmas?" It appeared that Todd had come around to Americana—he announced that he was listening to *folk music* on his iPod. Pete Seeger and "early" Dylan, music that his parents couldn't abide and had never played. Todd had explained, patiently, as if addressing clients who weren't sold on a particularly low-risk stock, that the loss of our "cultural roots" had much to do with the current social crisis. Elle thought that her son sounded like an imbecile. "When has there not been a 'social crisis'?" Elle had asked. America *was* a social crisis, and Elle went on to explain in what she knew was an equally pedantic tone that listening to folk music wasn't going to change that fact. But she didn't really argue with Todd; she knew him well enough to be able to predict how long his fascination with tradition would last— three months—for Todd, three months of paying attention to anything was remarkable. She often told her husband that their son had imbibed the spirit of the age in the over-priced schools he had attended. "He can't sit still or read a book or stick with anything." "Except making money," Elliot had replied. "He might have ADHD," said Elle, not believing it. Every young person born after 1980 had some kind of attention deficit disorder, due, Elle thought, to the arrival of MTV, instigator of the two-second attention span. She had grown up without television, forced, as her parents put it, "to make the most of her gifts." The truth was that Todd's habits were as much due to Elle's own preoccupations as anything in the so-called culture. She'd been only sporadically attentive to her son, especially when he was an adolescent, happy to let him go his own way so she could go hers. No matter, he was a fully functioning adult with business interests on three continents. What more could anyone want?

Elliot loved to point out that visiting family wasn't a game. Nobody was keeping a tally of visits made and owed. But Elle *was* keeping score— she always tallied up her obligations and weighed them against her actions. Visits paid, phone calls returned, letters answered in the proper order and in due time. "You can't stand being away from your work." Elliot offered her an excuse. "I can stand it, but I don't like to." She wouldn't say what the other thing was that held her at home. It wasn't Bethesda or Washington, their charming three-story brick home on Garrett Terrace. What kept Elle from visiting her son was her unwillingness to do something that had been asked of her. Saying no was a confirmation of her worth—it was that simple. She said no because she *could.* So Elliot would take a cab to Union Station and buy a coach seat and happily (Elle imagined him happy) ride up the drab edge of the continent while munching beer nuts and drinking a Coke—Baltimore, Wilmington, Philadelphia, Camden, Newark, then the long ride under the Hudson, emerging, as in Hopper's great painting, among the sooty brick apartments of mid-town. From the train window what you saw of these were dark tunnels, filthy gum-and-cigarette encrusted platforms, the smell of diesel fuel and piss, sumac trees rooted in garbage, the backsides of a thousand row houses. When she had been eight or nine her mother had taken her across country—New York to LA—on the train. Four days in a tiny compartment with Cristina, reading books and staring out the window at the immensity of the continent. Elle had been nauseous for long stretches; the train had reeked of disinfectant that was no match for the filthy toilets, excrement clinging to the steel bowls and—horribly—dropping straight down onto the tracks. Her mother had thought the trip rejuvenating, "We're like the pioneers." Never had four days seemed longer or more pointless. Elle couldn't bear sitting still for so long, the stifling compartment—it was summer and the train was airless. What was the point of all this scampering about? Italy too had been barren—dry and withered in the country, dirty and crowded in the cities. Why not be honest? Italy hadn't really appealed to her, not on her first or any subsequent visit. Recanati left her with a sense of privation, not unlike some of Leopardi's poems—a great emptiness leavened with yearning. Stunted trees, black-clad women—so many widows—dust, the smell of kerosene, motorbikes screaming through the narrow streets, leering men who followed her as she walked toward her hotel. No wonder the convent had appealed to Italian women—there one could be left in peace. Elle could feel herself sinking into lethargy on her visits, feeling heavy, eating too much, guilty because she wasn't happy in a place that should have felt like home. Or perhaps she'd been content and didn't remember—there was much she no longer remembered. *Scende la luna; e si scolora il mondo.* "The moon disappears and the world is colorless." There was that moon on her first night in Recanati. She had been a young woman, naïve, pursuing poetry, "searching"—she had written in her journal—"for the ghosts of the classical age." A romantic herself, she believed in ghosts in the way Mary Shelley or Charlotte Bronte had believed in "benign spirits." The dead leave traces of themselves that are perceptible to those attuned to the residues of the soul. Even now Elle couldn't disavow this belief. What was genius but permanence? Each time she worked on the *Canti* she sensed the presence of the mind behind the words. A mind: a collection of words, some shared with the world, some shaped into art, most kept secret. This had to be what she had felt, the ghostly presence—she still felt it. On a hill just outside of Recanti, as the sun settled and the moon followed soon after, a rim of white light in the northwest sky, there and quickly gone, the light taken from the surrounding hills covered with olive trees. She'd stumbled in the darkness, the evening, she remembered, had been cool—it was October—but she had been in no hurry to return to her hotel room, she strolled on the empty road, content to watch the black sky fill with stars. Leopardi often proclaimed that his life was ending—he said so, Elle believed, to provoke a sense of urgency. With his life waning there was good reason to work furiously, to cheat time. But the landscape would do this to anyone. Her mortality, his as well, felt more poignant in a place that had endured for so long. She thought all the while, "I am becoming a poet!" But believing in a correlation between experience and art was like believing in a connection between psychology and happiness: you might imagine there was such a connection, but it was only the believing that made it so. Elle might have remained at home, in a room like this one, and been a far better poet.

> *There was a time when we weren't who we are,*
> *When you and I were not like us,*
> *When we were lost, each to each.*

Though happy, we are forlorn. Could one be both at once? Leopardi was happy to be forlorn. A beautiful word, like the forlornness one felt at Provincetown in winter. Elle remembered the month she had spent in an otherwise deserted motel on the Cape, years before the Wellfleet house. She had meant to be there a week but the emptiness of the town and the foghorn skies and windy beaches were enticing, and she kept extending her stay, leaving only when she had run out of money. "Alone with her soul." Her *soul*, the tiny ghost, the small voice echoing behind her eyes, reason itself, the incarnation of the relentless march to the here and now. She'd felt it more on the Cape than any-where else. Felt it in the rush of foamy water up the sand, the air holes of mussels as the water receded. It had been the back and forth of the waves, the relentlessness of the water, the cruelty of it, that had put Elle in the mood for a soul. What, she had wondered (and written in a cycle of mawkish son-nets), did the eternal ocean have that she lacked? It was an idiotic question, but not an unreasonable one. Simple fact: in the presence of what appears to us eternal, we slip into kinship with what is eternal, pretending to understand what we can't. When Leopardi wrote about love he was pretend-ing. He knew nothing of women, though he felt the passion of a lover. Elle wondered how far feeling divorced from physical acts might take us in the direction of knowing love.

Elle thought about Cape Cod for several more minutes than she should have—the memory made her unhappy. "Why is that?" The poems were waiting. But when you tried to catch the tide, the roar of it on a bleak day, the smell (she could smell it here, in the dry, oceanless air of her study), what, when you came down to it, could you say that hadn't been said in "Dover Beach"? First rule of poetry: there's nothing to say. Second rule of poetry: everything remains to be said. Begin with those assumptions and you can't fail to write well. It was thinking you could say something no one had ever said before that led to trouble. Third rule: there are no rules, only genius. In music and in poetry there can only be genius. "Imagination is not characteristic of modern times…. Whose only source is nature…Supreme geniuses rapidly wear out their bodies and their actual mental facilities, their genius itself." (Pascal, dead at 39, already mad). Leopardi's body was worn out by the time he was the age that Elle was in the Sea Clipper Motel in Provincetown. Genius is self-consuming. Elle was grateful for her mediocrity. Her meager talents foretold a long life. Her husband had been a genius, but at one thing—a genius inside the open cavity of the chest. What, she had asked Elliot, had it felt like the first time he'd cut into a body and seen the heart, the beating heart? It must have been, she imagined, like looking into the center of the earth, or floating in the black empty silence of space—Elle had been much taken with the space program, not for its science, but for its poetry—"walking in space"—not only indescribable, but beyond the reach of language. And, it turned out, the living heart was beyond language as well since Elliot hadn't a useful thing to say about the experience of seeing one except for noting how calm he had been when he first came face to face with life's engine. How he'd empty his mind before he made the cut. "I just did it," as if he were shooting baskets or cutting the grass. Prose wasn't what Elle had been seeking; she'd hoped for insight, for a revelation that would make sense of the muck that was the body. How did we feel things, what was it about flesh and nerves that permit us to make and to appreciate beauty? "It was a man in his forties with the valves of a seventy-year-old. He died on the table." The mystical world of clogged arteries. If she could understand this one thing: flesh and beauty, neurons making Strauss.. The *Four Last Songs* were on the record player. Elle didn't remember putting them on; she was in the state of mind where putting on a record or drinking a glass of water didn't register.

Elle said aloud: *This can't continue.* You can't reprise your life day after day, making parts of it up, as if the story were someone else's. It was mad to do so—and she was becoming, she knew, her subject. Unfortunately, disregard for the truth is the basis of art. Art was a concoction, a splashing of paint, the labor of finding the right words to capture someone else's inner life, which, in time, became your own. Karl Richter becoming Bach ("No two performances can be the same, one goes beyond the written notes, one becomes the work.")

Desiderato il termine
Avrei del viver mio;
Ma spento era il desio
Nello spossato sen.

What was he saying? At that moment— deprived of love and happiness—*I might have wanted my life to end, but desire had died in me.* "But"? Elle wondered aloud if this was right. Is "desire" the desire to live or the desire to cease living? Does the loss of one sort of desire lead to the other? The dictionaries were no help—she knew what the words meant, but what had *he* meant? Did he think of taking his own life? No, of this she was certain. Like Pessoa, Leopardi had relished his suffering—it was his Muse. *Had all desire not died in me, I would have desired my life to end.* Death is desire—haunted yearning. Desire was killing him. There was something else. The crux

was desire—what was it? How had he felt it? Here
the gap between them was unbridgeable. Not love,
but life, the love of life, had driven him, that and
the desire for knowledge, which had been the same
thing—knowledge was life.

> I wanted my life to end
> but at that moment
> all desire had died in me.

Hours passed. The day began to wan before Elle understood that she was hungry. *Ravenous.* Strauss had ended hours ago—caught in the silence of the house, in the work, Elle had finally settled. There was nothing on her mind but the poems and, as often happened, Italian had become her only language—she wasn't translating but transcribing…

Outside her study, a mile away, two men were parked on the snowy shoulder of Route 34, their pickups nose to nose, arguing quietly about how much a man should pay to lease 100 acres just outside of Escabosa. In the drought, grazing land was getting expensive, though a cattleman willing to spread out his herd could still find acreage reasonably priced.

Two miles in the other direction, on the long, flat stretch to Moriarty, in a double-wide half a mile off the main road, a rusted hulk surrounded by cottonwoods, trucks and cars half-disassembled, kids' toys where there were no kids, a pile of cans and bottles that would never make it to the recycling plant, inside the messy narrow rooms, a man and a woman sat quietly at a Formica-topped table (gold sunbursts against dark brown) eating green chile stew and sipping ice tea. The man had a cigarette tucked behind his right ear—he was down to five a day—and the woman, dressed for her job at the chicken-packing plant, was eyeing the clock on the wall above the stove. They had four jobs between them. No kids, but they had plans for a family. "One thing at a time," Gustavo would say to his wife, "first a place of our own, then kids."

Next door to Elle, a mere half-mile across a flattened and snowy plain, Mrs. Lovato was stirring a pot of red. She too lived alone. Her sons were at the Air Force base in Albuquerque and would be coming for dinner with their families—eight people in all. A pot of red, tortilla dough on the cutting board ready to be rolled out, carne adovada simmering on the blackened wood stove, a gallon of sun tea half frozen on the porch. Mrs. Lovato had her radio tuned to KTQO and was enjoying the *ranchero* music she'd grown up with. It was warm in her kitchen, so much so that Mrs. Lovato had to open the door. She saw the wispy smoke coming from her neighbor's chimney and said a quiet "*Dios te salve*" for the crazy lady who walked about in the cold mumbling to herself, who never had visitors, and who never stopped in for *bizcochitos* or *posole* when invited. To be so alone was a terrible thing. Mrs. Lovato crossed herself and kissed the St. Joseph's medal that her sons had given her, clucked her tongue at the sparrows clustered around the jar of tea, and went back to her kitchen.

A light snow fell, then stopped, then fell again. The wind—you could set your watch by it—lifted dry powder onto the east-facing window of Elle's house. Ice-bound houseflies and spiders on the blackened glass. There wasn't a human sound to be heard. If you were walking across the great undulating field that divided Granite Knob from the highway you would see rabbit tracks and mosaics made by the snow, pellets of deer scat, dried leaves of elm and cottonwood. In other words, at this moment, this tiny sliver of the world was utterly serene.

Inside, oblivious to all that transpired around her, Elle was taking a break from Italian, reading her beloved May Swenson and waiting for the toast to pop.

Morning is a veil
sewn of only two
threads, one pale,
one bright.

Evening was as well, with the colors reversed. What time was it? The sun gives up early in January. Toast of two colors—burnt on one side, uncooked on the other. Apple butter put up in the fall from the trees inherited with the house. Russets, sour, pocked with worms, but serviceable for apple butter. There had been bees at one time—the hives stood empty and broken a hundred feet from the back door. In spring the worn path to the bees and clothesline and collapsed shed was eclipsed by wild strawberries, tart and deep red. The plum tree Elliot had planted still produced, but Elle left the fruit for the birds. That first year after Elliot's death she'd gone out with a basket and gathered hundreds of tiny, tart plums, but standing in the kitchen over steaming pots had felt pointless—why gather plums or apples for oneself? Cooking sustains social relations; she had none. She ate spongy wheat bread at every meal, hard-boiled eggs, frozen peas, cans of soup, pork and beans. It didn't matter any longer—reading poetry, Elle would be surprised to find her food gone—another task completed. Paying attention was becoming more difficult.

> "Streets will be   fields
>   cars be   fumbling sheep"

Why had Miss Swenson insisted on such structural eccentricity? Her poems shaped like George Herbert's—not churches and altars, rather wings and steeples of words, and these caesuras in lines that seemed not to have anything to do with the poem. Or did they represent rests, as in music, pauses for breath and for thinking? Or was it being a woman and a poet when women poets wrote ghastly rhyming couplets about doilies and dinner parties? Swenson was a tough broad—Elle thought she looked like someone who would brook no arguments. Toast in hand, she ambled back to her study, to Webster's Unabridged: *brook*, as in *brucan*. Which meant to enjoy. A lovely phrase. May had enjoyed no arguments. Elle wrote the definition out on a fresh pad. Akhmatova had shown how it was done, how a woman could make hard lines of poetry out of real feeling, how a woman could write about the great events that convulsed her world and not fall into mawkishness or sentiment. Nearly out of paper. Elle went back to her half-burnt toast. Anna meant "grace." A beautiful name. Elle's mother had preferred heavy meals, three times a day. Meat was consumed at luncheon (never "lunch") and supper. Rice and pasta. Fish as a first course served with beef. Her mother was rail thin, as was Elle, though she remembered her father developing a bit of a stomach. Perhaps he had fled for the sake of his health. "I grew up during the Depression," Cristina would say in defense of the family's astronomical food bills. Elle wondered if eating less due to economic and social catastrophe is what had led Americans to become gluttons. *Post hoc.* Imperialistic eating. She had read someplace about the American need for "regeneration." Uniquely among history's peoples Americans—Protestants in particular (so the argument went)—required periodic rebirth and reaffirmation. Though war mostly, but also massive consumption, exploitation of resources, oppression of poor people, a genocide now and again—yes, that too—no cannibalism, thank God. Elle had thought the argument was sad, though true. Miss Swenson would have had something to say about these subjects, though not in the volume Elle had carried to the kitchen. It was the poem about living in Florence that Elle had wanted: Each day's sky burned the Arno a different color. Older now, Elle could remember her room overlooking the river—the room, street, and river, all had been filthy, or had seemed so to a spoiled twenty-something-year-old whose concept of hygiene was formed in the suburbs. She hadn't washed for days at a time; she rinsed her face in a tiny sink whose effluent appeared to have risen directly from the river. Her damp underwear hung on the end of the brass bedstead, gray and melancholy. But a poet had to pay her dues, had to rinse out her underwear in a stuffy room overlooking a famous church—in her case the Basilica de Santa Croce where she sat for an entire afternoon considering the proximity of the bones of Michelangelo. She had been susceptible to genius in those days, eager to bask in the power of art, mad for the Greats, eager to read through the Canon, impatient to hear all hundred and one—was that right?—of Haydn's tedious symphonies. First genius, then nature, and finally the chastened self—those were the stages of her apprenticeship. All the while looking for the source of art, since all other meanings were lost. Staring at her empty plate—a few crumbs and a vague recollection of chewing—Elle thought again that she would never settle for irony, never concede a lack of significance. Of course history was a nightmare—only a fool would think otherwise—but here was Miss Swenson affirming that "Distance/and a certain light/makes anything artistic--/it doesn't matter what."

What it all means, Elle said aloud, what it means is that we grasp for life, greedy as starving dogs. And for starving dogs we might as easily feel pity as revulsion.

Elle put on the radio and looked in the refrigerator for something interesting. Expired yoghurt would have to do. As she sniffed at the lemony paste she remembered a cup of yoghurt she'd had on a train in France—a light mix of bitter-sweet cream served in a tiny stone pot she had scraped clean and then kept for forty years. Never, it seemed, had she tasted anything so delicious in her life. Was it a trick of memory or could she really recall the texture of it, the surprise she had felt that so ordinary a food could have suited the moment so perfectly? Was this, Elle wondered, a fitting topic for a woman her age—the memory of a casual snack? And if not, what was a fitting topic? There were many hours to fill each day, and the mind must be allowed to amble about as it wished. The train then, from Lisbon to Paris, through Basque towns and mountains—reading Proust and Lorca, daydreaming, half-sleeping in her coach seat, not anxious to arrive. Train trips were on her mind today. Flapdoodle. Of airline flights Elle remembered nothing—perhaps only the first flight, the one on which the pilot had to come back into coach and open the floor to manually crank the landing gear in place. Buffalo to Chicago in mid-winter, 1962. It had been a prop plane, and the pilot was wearing blue jeans and cowboy boots. Other than that, not a single viable image. Ditto car trips. She was in her kitchen spooning soured yoghurt into her mouth—no chewing required—and listening to a report on the government's bailout of Lehman Brothers. She had lost some money last year, a few thousand dollars that Elliot had put into securities—insecure securities. Money hadn't been Elle's strong suit—or Elliot's. They had invested in painters whose works never appreciated in value, in stocks that bottomed out during one of the periodic downturns, in companies that promised to develop efficient solar batteries, in drugs that Elliot thought would make millions—all losses. What, Elle had asked her husband, was the difference between investing and driving to the Route 66 casino? At least money lost at blackjack would go to the pueblo.

"That's just the way capitalism works," was her husband's reply.

"Meaning?"

"Meaning that you have to take some risks in order to profit. Nothing is guaranteed in this system."

"And that seems rational to you?"

"That's the *definition* of rational."

"Losing our savings is rational?"

"The recognition of luck is what is rational. Irrational people believe that if you do such and such then a predictable result will always follow. But life isn't like that. You have to factor in chance and mischance. If I perform a routine myotomy on a healthy patient I pretty much know what the outcome will be—90% of the time there will be a full recovery. But I can't ever be sure that something won't go wrong. Things go wrong all the time. Surgery isn't magic; neither is investing."

Elliot was fond of this kind of thinking—Elle called him the Last Rationalist—but in the end reason let him down. Elliot then reverted to his own brand of magical thinking. Capitalism, as far as Elle could make sense of it, was making the best of a person's worse qualities—it was the quintessence of magic: making gold from shit. The best poets hadn't worked for a living—no, that wasn't true. Stevens and Williams. Poets were like everyone else when it came to getting and spending—Elle's indifference was due to her dependency on Elliot. Now she lived on Social Security and Elliot's pension, more than enough money. Granite Knob was paid for—the house had cost less than a new car—and her needs were modest. Her son was rich and eager to send her checks—in fact he did send her checks on her birthday and at Christmas, but she never cashed them. What would she do with five thousand dollars? This was, she knew, her last stop—why complicate matters? What did it feel like to lose three hundred billion dollars? Or to have to write a check for that amount to save a company that was "too big to fail"? What was money? The desire for desire. "Everything is for sale," was another of Todd's opinions, perhaps inherited from his father. Also "The purpose of society is to bring buyers and sellers together efficiently." This kind of talk made Elle despondent. Even now, sipping peppermint tea and half-listening to an NPR story on another mass shooting—at a church in Charleston—Elle felt a wave of despair rise up at the thought of her son's narrow vision of the world. But, just as quickly, she shrugged—what difference did it make what Todd believed? What was a life worth nowadays? Not much, apparently. The anger spilled over daily—the victims were innocent—what was "freedom" but an excuse for brutality? Elle remembered a time when things were better, but then she wondered if she was imagining a world that had never existed. And what "things"? And better for whom? For her? Was life better for the fathers and mothers of the men and women murdered in the church, or had it been bad in a different way? It was better not to become sentimental. Elle admired Leopardi's refusal to substitute nostalgia for feeling—the

utility of melancholy, leveling out one's life, endur-
ing the persistent hum of sadness. The radio voice
that Elle usually trusted was saying that the President had acknowledged a targeting error, innocent
people, a wedding party, Pakistan—nothing to be
done—did he feel remorse? How many bombs had
been dropped since 1942, the year Elle was born?
Millions. Tests of atomic and hydrogen bombs,
fallout drifting east from Nevada, plutonium in
her milk—Cristina had made her daughter drink
coffee and club soda instead of milk to avoid Stro-
mium-90 so now her bones were brittle, her fingers
bent from calcium deficiency—in those days milk
came in returnable bottles, quart-sized, with a
paper tab covered by a piece of aluminum foil that
said Shorecrest Dairies, a skim of thick cream on
top, the bottle placed in an aluminum box by the
back door, the milkman wearing (Elle remembered
vividly as she sipped a glass of milky tea) an actual
uniform, a brown suit with a black bow tie, white
shirt and a cap—as if he were a cop or a fireman.
Elle laughed to herself at the surprising memory.
The milkman and the "black men" who drove the
garbage truck and walked around to the back of
the house to pick up the garbage—now Elle had to
drive to the dump on Wednesdays, right to the edge

of a trench filled with rotting vegetables and broken toys, the stench in summer fetid and sweet—and the school bus driver, a large woman whose name might have been Ruth, all of them got cigarettes at Christmas, cartons of Camels, yes, unfiltered cigarettes and maybe bottles of booze as well, wine for the black men, Scotch for Nelson—that was the milkman's name—and something cheap for Ruth, beer probably. Imagine giving liquor and tobacco to a delivery person these days, to the small Hispanic woman who delivered Elle's books—Elsa—a fifth of Wild Turkey, she'd probably call the police on Elle, alcohol as bad as abortion or gay marriage in these parts, hearty Catholics, with increasing numbers of Evangelicals—for some reason Elle's Hispanic neighbors had taken to the Pentecostal Church down the highway, a stuccoed A-frame fronted by an enormous cross and a billboard that pictured the crucified Jesus, blood running down his torn face and torso, stretched gaunt on a cross, obscene, "John 3:16" was proclaimed on a second, portable billboard, streams of cars and pick-ups on Saturday and Sunday and Wednesday filling the gravel lot, the minister a lean cowboy from Waco or some other Texas town that sprouted born-again Christians like alfalfa. The Catholics had gotten soft on gays and the services were (Elle knew from experience) tedious. Better to sway and shout and roll on the floor, *hallelujah*, better to have things clear. The cowpoke minister whose sermons showed up on KWIJ Sunday nights carried a gun into the tabernacle—his "sidearm"—and preached sexual abstinence in a town where fourteen-year-olds went to school *embarazada*—guns instead of sex, the church closed for a week in November during deer season, Reverend Carl calling hellfire down on liberals and the socialist president, a tired story, American resentment.

The milkman had faded, but Elle paid attention when the man on NPR said that Thomas Connelly had died of a heart attack, just that morning, in his home in Brooklyn. Elle had known Connelly—a handsome man, long-faced, whose elusive poems had turned her toward looser, more lyrical forms—toward a disdain for convention that reminded Connelly's readers of Neruda and Parra. Connelly had been prolific, publishing a book every other year, twenty in all, each one original, as if growing older only sharpened his perceptions. Elle began mentally composing a eulogy for Connelly, thinking that while she had been drinking her coffee in the dawn light he had been dying in another time zone. At what precise moment had it happened? Was it when she sipped her first cup—it was too hot—that his heart had stopped beating and the wind had left the sails of his lungs and his brain, just then busy writing a sonnet about dying, had shorted out, gone black forever? Time was odd, but odder still was the fact of contiguous events like drinking coffee and someone's dying. It was no longer unthinkable that a person might go mad simply by considering the strange juxtapositions of events—starving children and all-you-could-eat buffets. Todd scraping his plate full of unwanted vegetables into the garbage disposal; Biafran children lying, fly-covered, on straw maps, their bellies distended. Where did one go to find comfort in a world that allowed these two events to occur simultaneously? Leopardi had been wrong about religion—that it was based on fear and ignorance—wrong to miss the impossibility of living without hope. What did the truth matter? Leopardi believed in nothing else, but Elle had come to feel indifference to truth—where did believing that there was a way things really were get you? The way things really are is the way they seem to be at any given moment. There is no template of truth implanted in the universe or in the brain, a measure against which your compared your version of reality. The toast, the apple butter, the yoghurt and tea, this cold water, the light now aslant on the buffalo grass—and, Elle thought, this made-up person who has all the solidity of air or water, this version of Connelly on the radio…his life's greatest hits, all of which missed the man.

Elle finished up her tea and ate the last of the bread—perfect fare for a mad abbess—and rinsed off her plate. Poor Thomas. No more late lunches after hours of work, no more wine at dinner—he had been an oenophile of some renown, if one could be renowned for such a trivial achievement as wine tasting. No more sex. In New York and Boston Connelly had been a well-known man's man, and he'd broken many hearts. Elle hadn't ever slept with a poet, at least as far as she could remember. A photographer, but that had been fifty years before, a photographer who constructed collages from Polaroid snap-shots—ironic family studies—unattractive people, the deformed at play. Did one still say, "deformed"? Leopardi had been that—even his death mask showed a face and head not quite in proportion, but then who looked good in a death mask? Erik with a "k". He'd been lanky and walked about with two or three cameras around his neck—framing shots, making a little window of his hands every few minutes. He'd done that to Elle, framed her, as she lay nude on his bed. Unclothed anyway. She couldn't think of herself as ever having been nude. She remembered being upset, not wanting her backside to show up in one of his dreadful compositions. Later on, long after they'd tired of one another, Erik had been killed someplace in the Middle East, blown up by a mine or some other sort of bomb. Poets were sometimes killed in the line of duty, or languished in political prisons, or were sent off to die in exile. But mostly not. One's arteries hardened, one's heart grew weak from a lack of exertion—too much sitting—or, more likely, bad habits that led to cancer, the brooding disease. Elliot, Elle thought, had been lucky. She was hoping—if that was the right word—for something along the same line. Though not at mealtime. No question about it, Elle had taken less pleasure in dining alone than with her husband…what had she been thinking? Oh, about Thomas's house in Key West. She'd never been invited—they were casual acquaintances, having met half-a-dozen times at readings at the Library of Congress, once at the 92nd Street Y—she'd introduced him on a snowy night at the Folger— he'd read with Brodsky and Mark Strand—he read brilliantly, with real feeling, *chanted* his poems for nearly an hour in a rich baritone—she had been stirred, aroused—and years later, vacationing with Elliot in Key West—it was mid-summer, hot and humid, the beach had been empty, smelling of raw sewage—they had strolled each evening past the houses of famous writers—Hemingway's grand Victorian, Tennessee Williams's bungalow, Elizabeth Bishop's cottage—and found Connelly's house on Duncan Street, not far from Williams' place. She'd thought the house looked like it belonged to a writer—unkempt, overgrown with banana and mahogany trees, sable palms, day lilies—with a wrap-around porch for sitting at sunset—she'd wanted to stay forever—Elliot had been bored— bars and beaches and tourists made him feel like he was wasting his life. The house had been lime green. Elle could see it, standing (yet again) at the sink, looking at a landscape that suddenly seemed unbearably bleak.

She could leave tomorrow. Fly to Miami, rent a car, drive to the little hotel she had stayed in all those years ago—The Sandpiper—stay until spring, or longer, past the time of the winds, on into June, she had money in the bank, more than enough to last the next decade or so, "If I'm lucky," meaning lucky enough to make it to her eighties, and why shouldn't she? She was fit enough. Six months in Key West. Connelly had sold his house and moved to Brooklyn. The thought of Brooklyn, or of Thomas Connelly, or of having finally had a decent day's work made Elle feel a bit jaunty, as if she'd achieved something by being here and not there (and not dead). Confident. She didn't feel happy any more—happiness wasn't possible for a widow of seventy-three—but for just a moment she felt *lighter*.

A toast was in order. There were a few bottles in the pantry—she chose a nearly full Jameson Irish and poured two finger's worth. "To you," leaving the dedicatee deliberately vague—Connelly certainly, but also her poor husband, and her poet, her Leopardi. Down the hatch, warm and oaky, peaty, a rainy afternoon above the ocean at Dingle, waves breaking two hundred feet below, spume flashing, clouds blended gray to the west. When the whiskey hit—her stomach and head simultaneously—Elle had to sit. Heat flushed through her. She laughed: "Irish wake," thinking of one she'd been to, another dead poet, less famous than Connelly, but still, a published poet, a suicide, having hung himself in his office at the undistinguished university where he taught. Imagine finding him—he'd been a large man, "corpulent,"—the cleaning crew coming late in the afternoon for the trash, Gregory's face already purple (Elle imagined—she had no first-person experience with hangings), his trousers soiled, shoeless. Word had gotten to her in Boston and she'd gone to the funeral, paid her respects, "celebrated" Gregory's life and work. Not much of either, forty-some years, two slender volumes of incomprehensible verse, random sentences that bumped into each other for thirty or forty lines and then, as inexplicably as they began, ended. The first book had won the Yale Younger Poets and earned Gregory a stint at Yaddo—she'd been there herself, an interminable month—and a Guggenheim. The rest was murky. A bad marriage? Money troubles? There was something disturbing about the correlation between deep feeling and profound thinking. Elle remembered that Leopardi had believed the two were related. Poets committing suicide—no surprise there. Elle had no inclinations that way—"Whatever happens

at all, happens as it should" She didn't need to look
this line up—it was her single fixed belief.

Night

Just then, with Marcus Aurelius on her lips, there was a sharp pain in her side, not unbearable, but sudden and unexpected. Electricity spun from her brain, or perhaps an objection by her liver to the alcohol. She wasn't a drinker. The light was fading rapidly—Elle flicked on the fluorescent lights above the stove, brewed a second cup of tea. The worst hours of the day when you are alone—the cocktail hour and time spent cooking and eating with family. Light fading on the mesa, the sky not any color at all. Dead poets. Elle wondered if anyone would remember her, if the nice man on NPR's evening show would mention that she had passed away in a small New Mexico town, the highly regarded translator of poets….from…foreign languages. Would the taxpayers be willing to put up the funds for research and five minutes of national public radio on a woman who had spent her life on Leopardi and Saba, on the obscure post-World War I writers Elle had translated so many years before? She suspected that her case would be turned over to an intern—if that—and this intern would of course be illiterate and he or she would search for something on-line—was she on-line anywhere? Elle had no idea. And the result would be not much—a woman who wrote poems no one read and translated poems from Italian…that no one read. The denominator being the same in either case. Life divided by zero is still—is it zero or one? Either way. Who was reading poems when fifty million citizens lacked health care, when however many people were out of work or had lost their houses? Poetry belongs to high culture, to leisure and comfort, just like philosophy. No time now for mad pursuits. No, there wouldn't be a word on NPR or in the *Times. The Moriarty Shoppers Guide* included obituaries, but only of long-time residents, bean-growers and cattlemen, land-owners connected to the older families—the Lucero and Vigil and Gomez clans, people who had lived in the Valley for centuries, proud Hispanics (not

Latinos!) whose families dated back to the Pueblo Revolt. Not so terrible simply to fade away. Todd would remember her—as an odd and aloof old woman, not, she supposed, as the young mother who had spoiled him, taken him for long afternoon strolls on the Mall, to the merry-go-round in front of the red-brick Smithsonian, to the exhibits of colonial technology and the National Aquarium, with its stench of dead fish and chlorine. Who had stood him on innumerable Saturdays in front of the Rembrandt self-portraits in the West Wing of the National Gallery, who had lifted him onto her knee so that he could see the trailing smoke above the ferry in Eakins's *The Biglin Brothers Racing*, "Barney and James," Elle would patiently explain, "they beat all comers on the Schuylkill River, they were famous." And she would explain to Todd that Eakins had lavished patient detail on the background—the galloping horse, the fluttering red banners—because in those days paintings were pictures of the world, no cameras to speak of (not strictly true) and no TV. Todd wasn't interested, but he was docile. Next stop would be the East Wing. It was usually winter when they made these excursions, gray windy weekends when the city was empty of workers and the tourists were all at home watching football and eating casseroles. The best time to live in DC. You could get a table anyplace, find a cab, or, in Elle and Todd's case, a seat on the Blue Line. The vast cavern of the East Wing would be solemn with emptiness. There was the Calder, red rudders that Todd loved to imagine as part of a spaceship; the angles of the stairs that led to the great Morris Louis painting that inexplicably brought tears to Elle's eyes every time she saw it, or now, as she remembered it, all by itself in a dimly lit room, untitled, the unfurled colors seeming to creep along the edge of an otherwise monumentally empty canvas. "It's not anything you'd see, it's *just itself*," an idea that Todd accepted and that Elle worried over. Wasn't everything just itself? Why did these colors move her so? In Estancia, where Morris Louis was a distant memory—Elle had a book of his early work, but wasn't in the mood to get it out—the issue wasn't what Todd had thought of her amateurish lectures on art but on the stark absence of that world—the one where you'd wander through a museum, vaguely warm with the knowledge that it mattered to wander through museums—compared to the one she had come to occupy, the one where there were only words that might, if she were lucky, coax a bit of that other world to life. A muddle! Worse was the fact that her lessons hadn't induced a love of art in her son. No, art was only a "collectible," of the same order as antique automobiles and mint-condition stamps and coins. Elle had to admit that she was a philistine herself, an enthusiast rather than a connoisseur, too scattered to make a study of what she professed to value so highly. What did she really know of Eakins or Louis or Rembrandt? She owned biographies of all three but had never read them. It was tedious to read about apprenticeships and art schools and love affairs and rivalries. No scholar, not a poet, certainly not a writer or, God knows, a thinker. "It's the puzzles I love," and this seemed true, an avocation closer to accountancy than literature, balancing the books, sleight of hand. Another drink. This one a toast to her loneliness.

Night never "fell" in Estancia—it descended like a sinuous, opaque curtain, especially in winter. It felt like the earth had stored up the day's weight of sunlight and, as the afternoon waned, reluctantly gave it up. How little it took to make a world! Again at her desk, this time facing west, Elle marveled at the light, never the same light, photons or waves, what did it matter, somehow it blended with the flat brown desert and became, today, light sepia, toned in the inky secretion of a cuttlefish or refracted by sandstone and granite; tomorrow rose or watermelon, then the gray-green of snow clouds. Elle remembered how Kant had chided the empiricists for thinking we are passive observers of this magical world—recorders and not creators of these nuances, these minute variations, each of which possessed a name, each name a conjurer's trick, a category of memory that would help us to refine our seeing. Elle reached for *Zibaldone*—there was a post-it on the page—a passage she knew well:

In my theory of pleasure I describe how objects seen obscurely, or through a darkened glass, and so forth, evoke indefinite ideas in us, and through these ideas we can explain why, even when invisible to us, even when the source of the light is unknown to us, the light of the sun or the moon causes us to feel pleasure.

Indefinite ideas. Such as: what had she been doing all day? Here were the yellow pages torn from her notebook—fifteen in all—scribbled in pencil, in red and black ink. She'd finished four stanzas, five if she could fix a couple of words. Not quite the same as climbing into a caisson on the East River, welding door frames at Ford's Rouge River. She thought of the tour she had taken of the assembly plant, it was in the 70's when Detroit was still the capital of the industrial world. A cavernous building, a mile long, deafening noise, thousands of men and women moving around the chassis of gray metal, welding sparks. People dressed in blue overalls; she'd walked above the din on a catwalk, but then she'd never been to Detroit in her life and the only factory she'd ever visited was the Busch beer plant in Tampa, too long ago to remember a single thing other than the pungent aroma of hops. This was bad, this dreamy concocting of memories. Hadn't she enough actual experiences to fill her time? Did she need to make things up? Was she to become an unreliable narrator of her own life? At the first sign of dementia she would (she told herself) gobble down the Percocets she'd hoarded from Elliot's samples, years old, but surely enough to do the trick. Or, more likely, she wouldn't do it— she would hang on for as long as she could, adrift in the cold Atlantic, the lone survivor of the Titanic (her worst fear), she'd nonetheless grab the nearest floating object. Dusky thoughts. Sun fully set: always a moment fraught with doubts, especially since the day had passed so quickly and yielded so little. "A good day's work." What would that feel like? The weariness of finishing something tangible, watching the paint dry on a canvas. Exhaustion following a great burst of creativity; saving a life, saving her own. What did the Buddha do in the evening after he'd achieved enlightenment? A cup of tea with a grain of rice? Elliot was always ready for a Scotch after work—"taking the edge off"—and Elle had never blamed him. He'd been cutting people open, or, later in his career, he'd been sitting through endless meetings, writing reports, kissing asses. "Think I'll have a drink," he'd say as he walked through the door in Bethesda, as if there were a day when he wouldn't have a drink. Elle would be groggy from hours of reading and translating, staring through her magnifying glass at the compact OED, jotting notes to herself on index cards cut into bite-sized chunks: "*soavissimi diffusi*"=? or "mulberry leaves/drifting/funnels," the kind of notes she still wrote (these were from today), little questions or attempts at translations or pieces of poems she might write herself. Happy to be alone, pleased but disappointed that Elliot had come home an hour earlier than usual—"Why so early?"—not wanting to sound peevish, but annoyed nonetheless, eager to stop pawing through her dictionaries but reluctant to do so, certain that another hour would yield a breakthrough—to what? Not a stopping point since there was no stopping point. You didn't sew the poem up, stick it in an out-box, wash your hands and open a beer. The work was the life, and, so far, it hadn't ended, couldn't be tidied up at five o'clock—no quitting time. So Elle would join her husband for a drink—red wine—and half listen as he told her about his day, about the complicated lobectomy on the patient who'd been a coal miner for fifty years and had half a lung left—and lean toward her workroom, going over the last poems she'd worked on, the felicity of her late afternoon translations, the marvelous clarity that might not return tomorrow—stopping was a mistake—or, worse, her despair at having missed the mark again, everything she'd done since lunch was a mess, and she had her textbook editing to catch up on, her "real work" to get to, nothing was going well. And so it would go, day after day, never a break, no vacation. If she went to the Cape or to Annapolis for a "nice dinner" she'd be happy but miserable, unable to enjoy her lobster bisque, her crab cakes, thinking instead of Simone Weil renouncing food in London—she was reading Weil's essay on the *Iliad*—or just on edge, thinking of nothing at all. She'd been awful company much of the time, but Elliot didn't seem to notice. He ate his clam rolls and stared out the window at the boats moored in neat rows, watched the water-taxi ferry the owners of sailboats—the lucky few—from shore. Elliot claimed to wish that he lived on a boat, but Elle knew this was a childhood fantasy, nothing more. "You get bilious in a canoe," which was true: paddling on Lake Wallenpaupack years before, Elliot had vomited up his lunch. Life on a boat. A motorcycle trip across Montana. A pop-up camper. A cruise, of all things, through the Panama Canal. Elle had humored but thwarted each of her husband's fantasies, opting instead for a comfortable hotel in London or Barcelona, a long weekend in Paris when they were flush and Todd was away at boarding school.

And now, up again, to the window, to the kitchen table, back to the workroom—cold, so a heavier sweater, the sun fully gone, on go the lamps; the stove required attention—she'd let it burn to cinders—outside, quickly (wind!) for a few of the cedar logs cut for her by the nice man who owned the coffee shop and gas station, not him, his son, Roland, Ro, a strapping boy, robust, all bone and muscle, such a rush of things to do all at once, had she eaten anything since the toast? Should she think about a real dinner or work a bit more?

Somehow Elle had ended up on the kitchen floor, on her side, twisted awkwardly, lying on her arm, an ache arriving in distant capillaries—pinpricks. How? The wood she had fetched lay strewn about, some of it all the way across the room. She must have tripped, hit her head—it was throbbing, but there was no blood. She wasn't up to rising just yet. Instead, she turned onto her back, letting her arm and hand come back to life. Closed her eyes, perhaps she had fainted.

"I've fainted," saying so would make it true, but knowing as she said it that no, she hadn't fainted—she never fainted. "I haven't eaten a decent meal," not an explanation but an observation. There was a deeper pain just beginning, above her eye, sharp and visceral, she moaned, more to try out her voice, doing what she could to remember exactly what had happened. She had been rushing around, she was tired, undernourished. Perhaps concussed. Numb on one side. And wet. Odd. She'd never wet herself. She must have been unconscious for longer than she thought. It was dark as pitch, dark (Elle's mind wandered) as bitumen—"pitch" meant so many things. What good was English when the same word described a cricket field and a petroleum product? Elle started to push herself up—heading for the OED—but couldn't move. Something was wrong with her arm. Aloud, Elle said, "No need to rush. I can rest here for a minute." Her voice sounded deeper than usual.

The view wasn't terrible. Elle could see the bottom of her ancient oaken table—she had never been underneath it. As a child she had built forts out of blankets and pillows—reading forts—redoubts where she could be alone with her Nancy Drew mysteries. She thought of the secret lives of objects, the things we live with each day that we don't see and never think about. The ceiling was another matter. Elle noticed a new stain in the corner, just above the pantry—a brown map of India. She'd need to see about the roof. "Yet again!" The roof had been a source of contention while Elliot was alive. She'd wanted it replaced; he'd settled for patching. Husbands and wives: men with their delusions of knowledge, their false economies. She'd found it tedious to argue about the roof, the mice, the toilet that never quite flushed, always a bit of turd floating—his or hers, who knew—it was embarrassing. Elliot the former surgeon, he of the long thin fingers, the close-clipped nails, never had he wanted to dirty those hands, all of the household chores were Elle's, or farmed out, or left undone. Elle *quivered*. A thin pain shot from her shoulder to her pelvis, down her leg, then eased out of toes. Not, she hoped, a stroke, please. If she couldn't rise she'd die on the kitchen floor—no one would be checking up on her, not unless Todd flew in for a visit, and that wasn't likely. She'd be found, decomposed—the mice would feast on her eyelids—on her birthday, late in March, when Todd would, she was sure, drop by...Elle couldn't help but smile at the thought, Todd was as fastidious as Elliot. She visualized her son coming upon her corpse...enough. Up! Elle slid on her back toward her chair, grabbed the seat, and hoisted herself onto her rear. Not so bad. Her head hurt, her ribs ached. The sharper pain, the one that had cut deepest, was gone. She pulled herself to her knees and then, straining, to her feet, collapsing at once onto the chair.

"Well, what was that about?" Her slacks were drenched. She could smell herself—acidic, rank.

Elle was shaken. She badly wanted a drink of water but was afraid she'd fall again. She sat, thinking of nothing. Was this how it would end for her? Alone, collapsed on the floor or dead of a stroke in bed? She thought—I need someone to check on me—but she knew it wouldn't happen. Who would she ask, and, more to the point, who would she tolerate in her house? None of her neighbors save tradesmen had gotten past the front door. Elliot hadn't enjoyed the company of "cattlemen" as he referred to Estancia's citizens. A natural snob. And she hadn't protested—she was too old to make friends.

"Nonsense. I'm fine." Saying it made Elle feel better, and she pushed herself up, tottered to the sink and drew a glass of water—ice cold well water was, Elle thought, the cure for the "blues" as she thought of her "episodes." There had been others—she'd fallen before, fainted. Three times last year. Each time she'd worry about being alone, then have a drink of water and get on with her life.

She walked unsteadily to the bathroom, peeled off her clothes. There was a mirror, but she wouldn't look at herself. She wasn't vain, but there were limits. The prospect of a shower was inviting, but risky—if she fell in the tub, the heavy iron boat of a tub that had come with the house, well, that would be the end of her. Instead Elle wet a towel in the sink and soaped herself—she felt nauseous as she bent over to scrub her legs. She dried herself quickly, tossed her wet clothes into the hamper—a problem for tomorrow—and slipped into her bathrobe.

Full dark and bitter cold. Elle put the last log into the stove, and then decided she had to let the fire burn down, afraid to risk another trip to the woodpile. She had a cup of tea. Perched on the couch, curled up, staring at herself staring into the big window, nothing to see on the other side, a moonless night, stars, but invisible with the inside lights on. Looking at the window she saw herself, a tiny gray woman in an absurd pink terrycloth robe, slippers (from L.L. Bean), glasses on a lanyard dangling above a flat chest, circles under her eyes and frown lines and a sag beneath her chin, gravity pulling her back to earth. Elle stuck out her tongue, thinking that her body had both nothing and everything to do with her. Inside she felt not young, but certainly not old—she felt like a book of memories, opened to one particular page, one solitary instance of—how many was it, fourteen billion people who had been born and lived and died on this now wholly unilluminated earth—just one of countless numbers, hurtling around the sun, spinning like a top, and yet unmoving. The metaphor was irresistible—moving while sitting still, her heart beating a little too fast, her pulse like sand through an hourglass, pushing the pale skin at her temples. She might have been anyone, anywhere, and anytime—but no, that wasn't true, she could only be who she was here and now, a person with a particular history, with a set of hopes and failures issued at birth by her genes and a few circumstances—parents, country of origin, class— over which she'd had no control. No, it wasn't history that had created her, but accident, blind luck, the deck's shuffle. Her father, all those years ago, had been right. And what of his luck?

Standing now at the icy window. Ice. Her father's hand that last time she had seen him—she had lied and said his hand was warm, but it had been like ice. A week later the hospice nurse called and said simply, "His limbs are cold," and when Elle had been silent the nurse was more direct: "It won't be long now." Her father, her absent father, the one she could hardly imagine even when he was alive. Nothing about him had made sense to Elle—even strangers leave an impression, a sense of their presence as they pass through our lives. She could still hear his voice. But the man himself, the substance of the man, that had eluded her, what he believed in, what he thought about anything, what he liked. "It was as if he were waiting for something that never happened." She had tried to write about him, poems that were ghostly, empty of feeling. But that was only one of her fathers—the other one, the same man, was real to her, and of him she had visceral memories—two men in one body, as changeable as day and night, one she knew and one she'd never known. Elle sat back down—she was shivering and looked around for the blanket that was usually right on the back of the couch. How had that happened? Elle knew that it was her mother who had been the difference. Her invisible father was the man who lived with his wife. The other father, the one she had loved inordinately, had existed only for her, only when Cristina wasn't around, or on those rare occasions when she had been allowed to do something with him, just the two of them, the sullen little girl and the man who had at last come to life. Later on, after he had left, Elle would talk to him, to the empty places in the kitchen and living room she associated with him. He'd left hurriedly. She couldn't remember what she had said to the air—perhaps this memory was also a chimera—but she thought not. Had she asked him to come home, but wished, for his sake, that he would stay away? Oil and water. Her father had been water, Cristina oil, thick with being, full of demands, always unhappy. Why was that? Had Elle ever asked her mother the source of her discontent, her moodiness? Enough to drive away the man they both loved. Or was it her father whose airiness had ruined their lives? He'd been the sort of man who warmed to strangers—to bartenders and barbers, to whomever happened to be working at the bank or gas station—but who allowed no intimacy. Elle could easily imagine her father flirting with the nurse who held his hand that final hour. As for the business about intimacy, Elle knew that whatever failings her father had in this regard were related to his own father's disappearance. It was Biblical, this cyclic repetition of family sagas, each generation passing on the same curses, the same taste in clothes and alcohol. Elle had done what she could do throw over her father's legacy. She'd done her best to love those whom she was enjoined to love. Had she succeeded? This wasn't the time to answer such a question, though she already knew the answer. One thing she did know for certain--she'd loved her father deeply, loved him and hated him in equal parts. He'd been worthy of her hatred because he'd been worthy of her love. These matters of the heart weren't complicated, not any longer.

Elle snorted and sat down, disgusted with the thought of a ruined life. No one's life had been ruined. She had been sad for a while, and then she wasn't. Her mother, well, who could tell? And when her father came to visit—it was years later—he seemed perfectly normal, "himself," whatever that meant. What had she expected, a wrecked man, a ruined woman, a child's life destroyed by the perfectly routine discovery that a man and a woman might not be suited for one another? Who was suited for anyone? Had she "suited" her husband? What did Todd say about his mother to

Lucy? That she was distant and cold and far too rational to have succeeded as either a wife or a mother? Who was good enough for anyone?

Someone was knocking. Or not. It was difficult to hear anything in the dense quiet. Elle was startled. It was late. She went to the mudroom and turned on the outside light. There was a man on the front stoop—he was underdressed, wearing a sweatshirt. Elle thought, not for the first time, how strange it was that New Mexicans never wore proper clothing in the winter. Without a second thought, she opened the door.

"Yes? May I help you?"

"My mother had me come. I'm sorry to bother you."

He spoke with the accent of Hispanic New Mexico. A handsome man.

"I'm sorry. Your mother?"

"Mrs. Lovato." He gestured vaguely toward the road.

"Oh, yes. Of course. And did she wish something? A cup of sugar?" Elle smiled and pulled her robe more tightly around her neck. It really was cold.

"There was no outside light, no smoke. My

mother was worried about you." He was shivering.

"Here, please, come in. I'm sorry to be rude. It's too cold for you to stand outside."

The young man looked helpless, as if he wanted to walk away, but he stepped inside. Elle shut the door and walked toward the kitchen.

"I was just going to brew some tea. May I offer you some?"

"No, please, I need to go back. My mother is waiting for me. She wanted only to check on you, since you are alone, she thought...."

What, Elle wondered, had Mrs. Lovato thought? She'd hardly ever spoken to her neighbor, once or twice they'd met in the market, at the café, said *buenos dias,* a few Spanish sentences about the weather, their gardens, the bean crop. Elliot had gone to Mrs. Lovato's house on a few occasions to help out with chores—to cover the swamp cooler in October, to deliver a package that had been sent to them by mistake. Mrs. Lovato—she had a first name, but Elle had no idea what it was—had the worried look of a widow with too much time on her hands. Elliot had described her "possessing a Catholic sensibility," by which he meant (Elle had supposed), she expected the worst of the world. The world seldom disappointed.

"You're one of, what? Two sons? Gabriel and—is it Francisco?"

"Three sons. My brother was killed in Iraq. That was Gabriel. I'm Carlos. Francis is at house now with our mother. We work at the base and come for dinner on Sunday."

The military, a reliable employer in these parts. "I'm so sorry about your brother. It's a terrible thing, this war. And is your mother in good health?"

"Yes. She has diabetes, but takes pills. Thank you for asking. Anyway, I didn't wish to disturb you. My mother told me that you are a writer. That your husband was a doctor. My brother and I are grateful that you have helped her, helped my mother. It is difficult to be alone at her age. She won't leave Estancia to live with us. She won't leave her house."

Carlos sighed. Elle realized that this was a long speech for anyone who lived in these parts.

"I haven't done much. It was my husband. He and your mother got along. He was the outgoing one. I'm afraid I'm a bit of a homebody myself. I should visit your mother sometime."

Elle knew she wouldn't. Carlos seemed to know this as well.

The water had boiled. Elle filled the teapot

with leaves and water. Set out cups. Carlos looked askance at the tiny China cup.

"Perhaps you'd prefer coffee?"

"No. This is fine."

Elle poured the tea—too soon, it was weak—and sat down opposite her guest. It was strange to be seated at this table with a man who wasn't her husband or son. A man who, seated, holding a small cup in his large hands, bore a certain resemblance to Elliot, the young version of her husband, a slender and tanned Elliot who might have sat just so, hunched forward, sipping a cup of tea, looking into the cup for something to say.

"I guess your mother is a great cook?"

"Yes. Green chile stew, posole, carne. She goes all out for us."

"Sounds delicious. I don't cook much anymore. My husband did most of the cooking. He loved to putter in the kitchen. I've never been much for eating—I mean, I eat whatever is handy. I don't believe I've ever made posole."

"I will bring you some. With red chile. And beans from here in Estancia." Carlos smiled at Elle.

Eating with one's sons. Elle imagined that grace was said, the dead brother remembered, gratitude expressed for the food. In Spanish. Most of her neighbors spoke Spanish at home. The thought of a family meal was oddly comforting.

There were meals being cooked all around her. Families seated for posole and enchiladas, weak coffee and ice tea. Were there other women alone, not thinking of dinner, thinking instead of poetry? What did the other lonely women think about? Their dead husbands, if they had them. Their children, all of whom, it seemed, lived nearby, unlike Todd. Thinking about ways of not being alone, worried about their health, about passing out in the kitchen with no one to revive them. Was it so bad to be alone, to face every morning alone? What did the women do who had no work? Did they putter about their falling-down houses, tidy the family photographs yet again, dust the old piano that no one played? Elle had been in only two of her neighbors' houses. Both were wrecks on the outside—cracked stucco, dead rose buses, piles of paper and unstacked firewood, warped plywood sheds that held broken lawnmowers. But inside, the homes were pristine. Elle loved the smell of wood smoke soaked into the walls, worn hardwood floors, rough-hewn vigas, cast-iron stoves, quilts covering chairs and couches. Pride of possession. Elliot had said that the locals' Catholic faith inclined them to ritual, to worship. That possessions, however modest, were blessings. The home is a sanctuary. Preparing for the arrival of Elijah, for the pilgrim who would need a warm meal, a warm fire. Though there was no food, and the fire had been out for hours, and there were books scattered on every surface. A house that, in its vague disorder, resembled the contents of Elle's own mind.

"I need to go back for dinner," Carlos was staring at her—where had she gone? "My mother is expecting me. Will you be all right alone?"

"Yes, of course. I'll be fine. Thank you for stopping by to check on me. Please give your mother my warm regards. Your brother as well."

Carlos got to his feet and, for just a second, he put his large hand on Elle's shoulder, as if to insure that she was real. Elle shivered. When, she wondered, was the last time anyone had touched her?

"I'll stoke the fire before I leave."

"Thank you, it's all right. I can do it."

Carlos shook his head and walked into the living room. The big stove was barely warm. He reached into the kindling box and put a few cedar sticks into the firebox. He walked out the mudroom door and came in a moment later with an armload of piñon. Slowly, he coaxed the fire back to life.

Elle was touched by the attention this stranger was paying to her comfort.

"There."

The crack of cedar, the sweet smell of dry piñon. Warmth filled the room, a band of light shone on the threadbare carpet.

"Thank you."

Carlos smiled and gestured toward the windows.

"You should cover them. It will keep the cold out."

"Yes, but I like to look at the night."

"Suit yourself. Now I really must go."

Elle rose and held out her hand.

"Goodbye."

The house is quiet. The fire burns and cracks. The wind is now a low, steady drone across the front yard. It was odd how silence grew and subsided, as if it weren't absolute, on or off, one or zero. Elle imagined she could see Carlos bending over the fire. With her eyes half-closed she imagined again that he was Elliot, returned to look after her on this freezing night. In truth the two men looked nothing alike. But for just a moment Elle felt unalone, as if a man she didn't know and would never see again could take her husband's place.

It felt strange to have a visitor. Did men always offer instruction, admonitions, guidance? The officious castrato Abelard chastising Heloise in self-righteous letters—about her morals, of all things. Carlos was sent to check on her—did this make Elle feel safer or as if her privacy had been violated? Solitude, being unnatural, must be kept up full time, as devotion and a consistent practice. Elle, feeling a bit stronger, more "herself"—who else, pray?—returned to the kitchen for more tea, then back to the living room ("I'll wear out the floor!"). What would be best for day's end? Beethoven or Schubert? Chamber music, sonic chamomile tea to ease one into sleep. But Elle reached instead for the *Lieder* performed by Elizabeth Schwarzkopf, one of Elliot's particular favorites, Miss Schwarzkopf's voice like the trembling of leaves on a spring evening. *And man too will disappear*. Elle sat and listened, nothing more.

What was the question she'd been asking before her visitor arrived? There were so many questions that it was difficult to keep track. How about the one that required her to reconsider everything? What if, instead of living here, doing this, thinking that, what if she were to rearrange everything—to move, to give up on the *Canti*, to take up different opinions? She might become a nun, except for her lack of faith; or move to California, to some sun-swept city where she might live in a condo and walk her dog—a pug might fit her—on the beach. Nicely attired older gentlemen would comment on her dog, ask her to share an ice tea on the veranda of a plant-draped California bistro. She would decline, of course, explaining to her suitor that she was already taken, married, more or less. That was all right: this was California, it was the twenty-first century, no one bothered with monogamy any longer. No one—Elle's engagement with Schwarzkopf had dwindled with the opening bars of "*Die junge Nonne*,"—did a lot of things any longer. Read books, for example, or listened to Schubert *Lieder*. Or pushed in their chair (a pet peeve), or wrote letters. Progress, Elle said aloud, progress is killing us. An old refrain. Even if it were true that the golden age were over—and *when exactly* was the golden age?—it didn't matter a jot to Elle as she nodded off, slumping down at last for a nap that, for just a few moments, obliterated her consciousness. The record continued for one final *Lied*—"*Spute dich, Kronos*"—with the stylus unwinding through the final groove and, at last, rising with a jerky analog motion (not this or that but both at once) and a series of whirs and clacks that signified the end of an era.

Much later, the fire dying out yet again, the room losing its fragile heat, Elle's neck was contorted and aching. Asleep, dreaming of a trip—she was late for a plane or a train, or she was on the wrong flight, or, in some versions, she was running through what she knew, even in sleep, to be the old, crumbling version of Philadelphia's 30th Street Station (the Tribune Building adjacent), running in a wedding dress for a train that had already left the station. These dreams of being late were her daily fare now that she had seeped into old age. It was death, no doubt, that she was pursuing, that eternal obliteration promising to ease the ramblings of her mind. If she caught the train, then she wouldn't wake up. Even deeply asleep, Elle understood clearly enough the workings of her dream life. The voice-over (always in Italian) was Leopardi's, and his tone was chiding, hectoring, never solicitous. "*Presto.*" he would whisper, hurry, for you are late. An oddity of her dream life was not remembering anything that she dreamed, not even the parsing of images. All of her dream work was done while she was asleep, as if, in dreaming, her brain split into two halves, one craven and fearful, the other cold and analytical. Running toward something, or away from someone—tonight she favored the latter, and her disembodied dream voice asked, with all the clarity of dream talk, who it was she was running from, but, thanks to the collapse of the logs in the fireplace, she awoke before she had the answer.

Semi-awake. It was after nine, Elle's usual bedtime. Nine to five comprised her eight hours of rest, or, lately, nine to six, but so what? No time clock in her house, though she remembered when she had punched one as a teenager, working as a waitress—when was that? Sixty-one? Elle remembered—teetering on the verge of giving in to sleep right there on the couch—the smell of the kitchen—hot oil and fried meat—as vividly as if she were sixteen, dressed in black slacks and a white shirt, wearing a green apron, clutching a pad for orders, refilling mugs of coffee. The boss had grabbed her ass as she scuttled from the storeroom to the waitress station with an armload of napkins—Mr. Pallini or maybe Padidini. The one and only time she could recall being groped—sexually assaulted. She'd gone home and told her father, who in turn spoke to the three hundred pound Pallini. What was said was anybody's guess. Her father hadn't an aggressive bone in his body, though he had a temper and wouldn't let anyone get away with abusing his daughter. Anyway, that had been the end of Elle's waitressing career, and, come to think of it, of her summer jobs. After that she'd signed up for summer classes and lounged around the house. Which was what she was doing these days—resting up for older age. Never had she ever worked in a way that would induce fatigue—mental work, housework, play work. She'd been idle for much of her life, turning around sentences, living vicariously. Anyway, Elle disbelieved in actual freedom of the will, as in that she might have gone into waitressing for the long haul, or litigation, defending the victims of priapistic men, or decided to marry her childhood sweetheart, if she'd had one. Had she? The truth was, she was worn to a nub, exhausted from the effort of unsatisfactorily translating half (less!) of one of Leopardi's poems. She hauled herself up from the couch and went into the downstairs bathroom to brush her remaining teeth—no, she hadn't cared for them, hadn't flossed or gone twice yearly for check-ups, she'd been too busy and as a result had a mouth full of gaps and bridges. Too busy for her teeth and annual pap smear and breast cancer screening and for decent hair cuts, pedicures, massages, or colonoscopies—nor had she bothered to

pay her taxes since Elliot died and took his knowledge of accounting with him, nor had she joined a
gym—of which there were none in Estancia—voted
in a local or national election, sent money to St.
Jude's Children's Fund (as she once had), attended
church, confessed her sins, or thought for even a
second about her immortal soul. No, she'd been busy
with a long-dead Italian genius and with assembling
and reassembling the jig-saw puzzle of her unremarkable past. She did, at least, gargle, enjoying
the warm cycling of salty water on her tonsils—yes,
she had them still, and her appendix, though her
father had nearly died in his thirties when his burst,
without warning, on a family car trip to the Adiron-
dacks. He'd collapsed in the lobby of a cheap motel
in some tiny upstate town; the ambulance had to
rush him to Cortland for surgery. Teeth, hair, hearing, sense of taste—well, those were a lost cause,
but she knew neighbors far younger than she who
had lost kidneys and ovaries, who shot up insulin
every few hours, a handful who'd survived chemo
and a larger handful who hadn't. All in all, for an
old lady—not so very old—she wasn't doing badly.
Aches and pains, fainting spells, random collapsing and losing consciousness—all part of the drill.
The stairs up to her bedroom—not the marital

bedroom, the "master" bedroom that took up the entire back end of the house, with its sleeping porch and walk-in closet (still full of Elliot's clothes since Elle hadn't the heart to bag them up for the Vietnam Vets)—not that one, too painful, but the small guest bedroom that had gone almost entirely unused until Elle moved her own clothes and books into it the week after Elliot died. The room was wallpapered in golden asters, and the floorboards, wide as the planks on a sailing ship, creaked and moaned through the night, expanding and contracting, or, as Elliot would have it, "settling"—"You mean sinking"—into its hundred-year-old foundation. An icebox at this time of year, heated only by the rising warmth of the living room stove. But Elle didn't mind the cold once she was buried under her quilts and comforters, their goose down warmed her, and she imagineded her bed a kind of launching pad for dreaming, her nights replete with images that, upon waking, Elle would forget entirely, or make up out of someone else's dreams. Making things up was mostly what Elle was up to these days.

⌇

Her nightly rituals complete—teeth and hair brushed, bladder emptied (she flushed for the first time that day, water being perennially scarce), bra and underwear washed out in the sink, cotton nightgown (it smelled of sweat and talc) pulled on, robe cinched tight—Elle thought she might make one last visit to her desk, not to work, but to tidy and prepare for the morning. First a glass of water for her bedside, check the lock on the back door, stove cooling, lights switched off. Oh how pleasant the simple things can be, how refreshing to wander from room to room with no particular purpose aside from housewifery. At the same moment she also thought how dreadful it was to be alone in this large and drafty house, and she cursed her husband for abandoning her in such a place. Aloud, Elle said: "No more fussing about this life of mine." Saying this little prayer, she felt much better.

Her desk was untidy, but efficiently so—she'd be able to pick up work in the morning at the point she had left off in "Il Risorgimento." Standing above her books, she tried the stanza without thinking about accuracy—"Bereft of sweetness, sad but unperturbed, my being/self was calm, and my glance was serene." Lovely, but then this: *Desiderato il termine/ Avrei del viver mio*. Elle shivered as the line unfolded, the logic hard as steel: why not die since you are feeling so good? But then, in typical Leopardi fashion, the macabre irony—*Ma spento era il desio….*" anyway, I've no desires any longer, my feelings are gone, so, Elle added a coda herself—why not tarry, live on Giacomo! And so he had, though not a great deal longer. The cult of misery, so romantic, responsible for great poetry and ghastly politics. The fascists were also romantics, strutting ninnies saluting their *Duces*, all of them with their grotesque worship of annihilation, the ultimate in sensation for men who had staked everyone's future on the perversity of emotion. Sickened by reason, what was left but destruction? And if you had an army at your disposal, why not destroy everything? The deep thinkers also love death, but straight up, without pretense, without believing their self-annihilation means anymore than what it is—an ending, not an apotheosis. Had Leopardi killed himself Elle wouldn't have wasted a second on his poetry. It was life that she wanted from her beloved Italian, not death.

Elle closed the *Canti* and put away her yellow legal pads, stored her pens. The thought of taking a break crossed her mind again—it had been the day's theme. Maybe she would. She'd been thinking of driving to Juarez. It would be warmer there, and she loved walking around the market and sitting in the Cathedral. The city wasn't safe—she knew that—but where was one safe any longer? She thought she'd pack her suitcase right now and get an early start in the morning, but by the time she had reached her bedroom the idea of going to Mexico had vanished. Instead she turned on her reading lamp and sorted through the mysteries that lulled her to sleep each night. Nothing appealed. Oddly enough, she found herself kneeling by her bed, her head bowed, weeping. For a moment she let herself go, she felt herself tipping from tears to sobs, and then, just as quickly as her sadness compelled her to kneel and cry, she felt nothing but tired. Blank and ghostly, she walked to window, raised the shade, and looked up. It was a moonless night, and on Granite Knob the band of stars that comprised the edge of the Milky Way was clearly visible. She concentrated for a moment on the oddity of so much emptiness, but was too worn out to feel anything more. Nothing left but to end the day, and, with luck, to rise again in the morning, to see what would come to her for all the days she had left.

ACKNOWLEDGMENTS

I am deeply indebted to Iris Origo's *Leopardi: A Study in Solitude*, first published in 1953 and reissued by Helen Marx Books in 1999.

To Michael Caesar's brilliant edition of Leopardi's *Zibaldone*.

For the *Canti*, I relied on Jonathan Glassi's, Frederick Townsend's, and Eamon Grennan's renderings of the poems. Glassi in particular seems to me to have come as close to perfection with these brilliant songs.

May Sarton's *Journal of a Solitude* deserves to be better known and helped me immensely.

Marc Estrin and Donna Bister: thank you for everything.

There is a lovely little town named Estancia east of where I live; I have visited it many times. However, that town bears no relation to the place portrayed here.

Peter Nash and Michael Keith encouraged me when I needed it most.

David Gutierrez and Chris Pietsch—comrades and friends.

My daughters—Alexis, Dorothy, Ada—give me hope.

George Ovitt is the author of two collections of poetry, a book of short stories, and a work of history. He is the co-author of the popular literary blog talentedreader. He lives in New Mexico.

About Fomite

A fomite is a medium capable of transmitting infectious organisms from one individual to another.

"The activity of art is based on the capacity of people to be infected by the feelings of others."
—Tolstoy, *What Is Art?*

Writing a review on Amazon, Good Reads, Shelfari, Library Thing or other social media sites for readers will help the progress of independent publishing. To submit a review, go to the book page on any of the sites and follow the links for reviews. Books from independent presses rely on reader to reader communications.

For more information or to order any of our books, visit
http://www.fomitepress.com/FOMITE/Our_Books.html

More Titles from Fomite...

Novels
Joshua Amses — *Ghatsr*
Joshua Amses — *During This, Our Nadir*
Joshua Amses — *Raven or Crow*
Joshua Amses — *The Moment Before an Injury*
Jaysinh Birjepatel — *The Good Muslim of Jackson Heights*
Jaysinh Birjepatel — *Nothing Beside Remains*
David Brizer — *Victor Rand*
Paula Closson Buck — *Summer on the Cold War Planet*
Dan Chodorkoff — *Loisaida*

David Adams Cleveland — *Time's Betrayal*
Jaimee Wriston Colbert — *Vanishing Acts*
Roger Coleman — *Skywreck Afternoons*
Marc Estrin — *Hyde*
Marc Estrin — *Kafka's Roach*
Marc Estrin — *Speckled Vanities*
Zdravka Evtimova — *In the Town of Joy and Peace*
Zdravka Evtimova — *Sinfonia Bulgarica*
Daniel Forbes — *Derail This Train Wreck*
Greg Guma — *Dons of Time*
Richard Hawley — *The Three Lives of Jonathan Force*
Lamar Herrin — *Father Figure*
Michael Horner — *Damage Control*
Ron Jacobs — *All the Sinners Saints*
Ron Jacobs — *Short Order Frame Up*
Ron Jacobs — *The Co-conspirator's Tale*
Scott Archer Jones — *And Throw the Skins Away*
Scott Archer Jones — *A Rising Tide of People Swept Away*
Julie Justicz — *A Boy Called Home*
Maggie Kast — *A Free Unsullied Land*
Darrell Kastin — *Shadowboxing with Bukowski*
Coleen Kearon — *Feminist on Fire*
Coleen Kearon — *#triggerwarning*
Jan Englis Leary — *Thicker Than Blood*
Diane Lefer — *Confessions of a Carnivore*
Rob Lenihan — *Born Speaking Lies*
Colin Mitchell — *Roadman*
Ilan Mochari — *Zinsky the Obscure*
Peter Nash — *Parsimony*
Peter Nash — *The Perfection of Things*
Gregory Papadoyiannis — *The Baby Jazz*

Pelham — *The Walking Poor*
Andy Potok — *My Father's Keeper*
Kathryn Roberts — *Companion Plants*
Robert Rosenberg — *Isles of the Blind*
Fred Russell — *Rafi's World*
Ron Savage — *Voyeur in Tangier*
David Schein — *The Adoption*
Lynn Sloan — *Principles of Navigation*
L.E. Smith — *The Consequence of Gesture*
L.E. Smith — *Travers' Inferno*
L.E. Smith — *Untimely RIPped*
Bob Sommer — *A Great Fullness*
Tom Walker — *A Day in the Life*
Susan V. Weiss —*My God, What Have We Done?*
Peter M. Wheelwright — *As It Is On Earth*
Suzie Wizowaty — *The Return of Jason Green*

Poetry

Anna Blackmer — *Hexagrams*
Antonello Borra — *Alfabestiario*
Antonello Borra — *AlphaBetaBestiaro*
Sue D. Burton — *Little Steel*
David Cavanagh— *Cycling in Plato's Cave*
James Connolly — *Picking Up the Bodies*
Greg Delanty — *Loosestrife*
Mason Drukman — *Drawing on Life*
J. C. Ellefson — *Foreign Tales of Exemplum and Woe*
Tina Escaja/Mark Eisner — *Caida Libre/Free Fall*
Anna Faktorovich — *Improvisational Arguments*
Barry Goldensohn — *Snake in the Spine, Wolf in the Heart*

Barry Goldensohn — *The Hundred Yard Dash Man*
Barry Goldensohn — *The Listener Aspires to the Condition of Music*
R. L. Green — *When You Remember Deir Yassin*
Gail Holst-Warhaft — *Lucky Country*
Raymond Luczak — *A Babble of Objects*
Kate Magill — *Roadworthy Creature, Roadworthy Craft*
Tony Magistrale — *Entanglements*
Andreas Nolte — *Mascha: The Poems of Mascha Kaléko*
Sherry Olson — *Four-Way Stop*
David Polk — *Drinking the River*
Aristea Papalexandrou/Philip Ramp — *It's Passing Us By*
Janice Miller Potter — *Meanwell*
Philip Ramp — *The Melancholy of a Life as the Joy of
Living It Slowly Chills*
Joseph D. Reich — *Connecting the Dots to Shangrila*
Joseph D. Reich — *The Hole That Runs Through Utopia*
Joseph D. Reich — *The Housing Market*
Joseph D. Reich — *The Derivation of Cowboys and Indians*
Kennet Rosen and Richard Wilson — *Gomorrah*
Fred Rosenblum — *Vietnumb*
David Schein — *My Murder and Other Local News*
Harold Schweizer — *Miriam's Book*
Scott T. Starbuck — *Industrial Oz*
Scott T. Starbuck — *Hawk on Wire*
Scott T. Starbuck — *Carbonfish*
Seth Steinzor — *Among the Lost*
Seth Steinzor — *To Join the Lost*
Susan Thomas — *The Empty Notebook Interrogates Itself*
Susan Thomas — *In the Sadness Museum*
Paolo Valesio/Todd Portnowitz — *La Mezzanotte di Spoleto/
Midnight in Spoleto*

Caitlin Hamilton Summie — *To Lay To Rest Our Ghosts*
Susan Thomas — *Among Angelic Orders*
Tom Walker — *Signed Confessions*
Silas Dent Zobal — *The Inconvenience of the Wings*

Odd Birds

William Benton — *Eye Contact*
Micheal Breiner — *the way none of this happened*
J. C. Ellefson — *Under the Influence*
David Ross Gunn — *Cautionary Chronicles*
Andrei Guriuanu and Teknari — *The Darkest City*
Gail Holst-Warhaft — *The Fall of Athens*
Roger Leboitz — *A Guide to the Western Slopes and the Outlying Area*
dug Nap— *Artsy Fartsy*
Delia Bell Robinson — *A Shirtwaist Story*
Peter Schumann — *Bread & Sentences*
Peter Schumann — *Charlotte Salomon*
Peter Schumann — *Faust 3*
Peter Schumann — *Planet Kasper, Volumes One and Two*
Peter Schumann — *We*

Plays Stephen Goldberg — *Screwed and Other Plays*
Michele Markarian — *Unborn Children of America*

Essays

Robert Sommer — *Losing Francis*